MERCY HOSPITAL
CRISIS!

Look for These Other
MERCY HOSPITAL *Books*
Coming Soon from Avon Camelot

THE BEST MEDICINE
DON'T TELL MRS. HARRIS

MERCY HOSPITAL
CRISIS!

CAROLYN CARLYLE

AN AVON  CAMELOT BOOK

MERCY HOSPITAL: CRISIS! is an original publication of Avon Books. This work has never before appeared in book form.

AVON BOOKS
A division of
The Hearst Corporation
1350 Avenue of the Americas
New York, New York 10019

Copyright © 1993 by Seth Godin
Published by arrangement with Seth Godin Productions
Library of Congress Catalog Card Number: 92-97005
ISBN: 0-380-76846-1
RL: 5.4

First Avon Camelot Printing: February 1993

CAMELOT TRADEMARK REG. U.S. PAT. OFF. AND IN OTHER COUNTRIES, MARCA REGISTRADA, HECHO EN U.S.A.

Printed in the U.S.A.

OPM   10   9   8   7   6   5   4   3   2   1

With deepest thanks
to the hundreds of thousands
of Junior Volunteers in hospitals nationwide

Contents

1

The Great Job Hunt

"Earth to Nichole!" Bernadette O'Connor, her green eyes narrowed and her freckles stretched across a broad grin, studied her pretty friend. "Nichole Peters, you're boy-watching again!"

But Nichole didn't answer. Instead, she continued to focus all her attention on the football player two tables away in Ridge Dale High's sprawling, noisy cafeteria. "Doesn't Brian Stone have the most heavenly eyes in the universe?" she asked, running one hand over her honey-colored hair, even though not a single strand was out of place.

The small brunette next to Nichole stopped chewing her burger and waved her hand in front of their friend's face. "It's no use, Bernie," Shelley Jansen announced. "She's tuned us out." She nodded toward the handsome profile and broad shoulders of the upper classman.

"When it comes to boys, Nichole can't see anything else—even her two best friends!"

The lively redhead laughed. "As one of those best friends, do you think I should break it to our full-time flirt that Brian is the most popular boy in school and we're just lowly freshmen?"

"Freshmen." Shelley repeated the word, glancing around the bustling room. "I don't *feel* like a freshman," she said, pushing her dark french braid back from one shoulder. "I'm already at home here."

"I know what you mean," Bernie agreed. "We've only been in high school a few months, but I can't imagine having more fun." She smiled with affection at the two girls across the table from her. "Or more terrific friends." She picked up a soggy french fry from the plate on her tray, then let it drop. "But I *can* imagine better food!"

"Hey, did I hear someone joking about our school's fine cuisine?" asked a tall, lanky boy with his hair shaved in the latest punk style. "That's my job!"

Teddy Hollins, a far-out, funny freshman, folded his skinny legs like a jackknife as he sat down beside Bernie. "Mind if Roger and I join you, ladies? Basking in your beauty will make it easier to face the cafeteria's Thursday special!"

Teddy made a career out of dressing and talking outrageously, never letting his friends see his serious side. "Greetings, Mr. Hollins," Bernie teased him right back. "I take it grease burgers aren't your favorite Ridge Dale treat."

"I don't know," Teddy told her, shrugging. "It's so hard to choose a favorite." He counted days off on his

2

fingers. "Monday, it's poison pizza. Tuesday, it's toxic turkey. Wednesday, it's nightmare stew . . ."

"Stop, you're making me hungry!" Laughing, a second boy joined them at the table. Sandy-haired with gray eyes, Roger Thornton had a friendly, quiet manner and the sturdy body of a born athlete. He was as different from Teddy as any boy could be, yet the two were the closest of friends.

"Hi, Roger." Nichole beamed her perfect smile at the newcomer, ignoring Teddy. "You play football, don't you?" She looked at him slyly, her blue eyes full of plans. "Can you introduce us to that heavy-duty hunk over there?" She pointed to Brian, then winked at Shelley and Bernie.

Roger, already a standout quarterback on the freshman squad, laughed good-naturedly. "I'm only on the freshman team, Nichole," he told her. "I don't really know Brian. Besides, doesn't he already have a girlfriend?" He nodded toward the pretty girl sitting beside the football star.

Nichole, the headstrong daughter of one of Ridge Dale's wealthiest families, was always aiming high. Her friends were used to her impossible crushes on movie stars, rock singers—and now, on Ridge Dale's football captain. She studied the slender girl who was talking with Brian and his friends. "Her? That's just Mariah Tecknor. She couldn't be dating anyone as awesome as Brian Stone."

"Why not?" asked Bernie. "Mariah's in my Bio class. She seems really nice." The teacher in Bernie's special Honors class was always calling on Mariah, and Mariah always knew the answers. But Bernie noticed

3

that the friendly senior never acted stuck-up or conceited.

"I've met her," said Shelley, recognizing Mariah. "That's the girl who helped me on the first day of school. I was trying to find the language lab and I ended up in the chorus room instead!" She laughed, remembering how confused she'd been trying to find her way through four floors and hundreds of milling students. "She was really friendly."

"But that's exactly what I mean," protested Nichole, staring again at the slim brunette beside Brian. "Mariah's nice to everyone, she sings in the chorus, works on the Community Service Club, and gets straight A's." She crinkled her pretty nose in disgust. "How boring can you get?"

"Careful there, Nick," Bernie warned her, smiling. "As I recall, you once thought I was a boring brain, too."

"That was before I got to know you," Nichole told her new best friend. She grinned innocently, her huge blue eyes blinking like a baby doll's. "Somehow *you* manage to get great grades and still be fun."

"Thanks, I guess." Bernie laughed. She knew Nichole's parents, famous architects, gave her everything she wanted, and she knew her pretty friend had little patience for hard work. But even though Nichole was flighty and spoiled, Bernie couldn't help loving her. Underneath that moussed hair, inside those fabulously expensive clothes, there was a tender, funny girl.

"I hope you've changed your mind about me, too, Nichole." Shelley's deep chocolate eyes were full of mischief. "Remember the day you met me?" She would never forget her first Home Ec class at the high school,

4

the way she'd raced out into the hall after her corn soufflé had gone up in smoke. Her hair had been singed, her face and clothes had been covered with grease, and the first person she'd bumped into was a Barbie Doll look-alike!

"You were disgusting!" Nichole remembered the soot-covered ragamuffin who had nearly knocked her over in the hall. "You told me it was an emergency, and you were right. Your clothes were a disaster and your hair was worse."

"The emergency was the fire I'd started," Shelley insisted, "not my grooming."

"If you ask me," Nichole said, remembering how Shelley's face had been smeared with long black stains, "it was both!"

"I'm afraid," Bernie announced, putting a hand on each girl's shoulder, "we've got another emergency on our hands." She looked from one of her friends to the other. "Or have you forgotten our job crisis?"

Shelley and Nichole stopped their mock quarrel and groaned. Shelley slumped in her chair. "Don't remind me," she complained. "I combed the *Ridge Dale Reporter* last night after dinner. There's not a single job that any of us is qualified for."

"That's right," Nichole moaned, looking suddenly serious. "This morning fat old Mrs. De Vichio in the Guidance Office had the nerve to tell me she wouldn't even give me a work permit."

"That's because she can't," Roger explained to her, leaning across the polished table to make himself heard in the noisy room. "You can't get one until you're fifteen. It's the law."

"Then how am I supposed to get a job?" wailed

Nichole, sounding like the tragic heroine of an old movie.

"Just why do you need a job at all, Foxy Lady?" Teddy asked. He wore a heavy metal T-shirt and a diamond chip in one ear, but his cool was only skin deep. Around Nichole, he usually turned to jello. "Your parents have enough money to buy the whole town."

"Daddy says I need the experience," Nichole told him, her voice trembling as if the world were ending. "He says unless I find work, he's going to cut my clothes allowance."

"It's a lot worse for me," said Shelley. "My dad's decided it's time I started helping out with family expenses. And when my dad decides something, he means business." Mark Jansen, Shelley's father, was a divorced single parent who managed the night shift at a local factory.

Bernie knew that Shelley's home life was very different from her own. Shelley's mother was a recovering alcoholic who had moved to California and almost never visited her family. Her dad worked such long, hard hours that Shelley hardly saw him except on weekends. Bernie, on the other hand, couldn't imagine not sitting across from both her parents' cheerful faces at the dinner table each night. Although last night, she had to admit, Mr. O'Connor hadn't looked that cheerful at all.

"My dad's cracking down, too," she told her friends. "In fact," she added gloomily, "it looks like I won't be able to talk on the phone anymore."

"What?" The two boys and two girls at Bernie's table asked the question in unison. After all, the five of them had already become such good friends that they spent hours on the phone every night.

6

"I'm serious," Bernie told them. "My folks are really uptight lately." She shook her head, trying to figure her parents out, then gave up. "Ever since you talked me into piercing my ears, Nick, they act like they expect me to elope or shave my head any minute!"

Nichole shrugged. "How did I know you weren't going to get their permission first?" she asked. "Besides," she added, smiling mischievously, "you definitely look hot."

"Agreed," confirmed Teddy. "Almost as hot as Mr. Suave himself." He turned his head, proudly displaying the diamond stud in his own left ear.

"Hot or not," Bernie laughed, "it looks like I'm really on hold, as far as the telephone goes." She remembered last night's family conference, her dad's awful speech about how disappointed he and her mom were. "My folks say that since school started, I've been spending less and less time with the family and my books and more and more time on the phone." She could still see her father's serious expression. Mary and Frank O'Connor weren't the kind of parents who needed to yell to make their point; all it took was that sad you-let-us-down look in their eyes.

"You mean I can't call you to find out what you're wearing in the morning?" Nichole looked devastated.

"I can't put Clarisse on the phone anymore?" Shelley, who spent most of her evenings alone, liked to call Bernie just before she went to bed. That's when she'd let her fat tabby cat purr into the receiver to say good night.

"I can't play you my latest pick hit?" Teddy had the largest CD collection in their group, and he insisted that his friends spend hours listening to his newest recordings.

"How about just calling to say hi?" Roger looked confused. "Is that off limits, too?" It was clear from his expression that he was even more upset than the rest of Bernie's friends.

"I guess not." Bernie smiled at him fondly. "It's just that I'm going to have to really cut back. Maybe if we can find jobs and I can prove I'm responsible, things will be different."

"Wait just a minute! A teenager who's giving up the phone?" Teddy pressed his two hands around an imaginary camera. "Let me grab the old air camera. I've got to get this on film!"

"Normal people play air guitars," Nichole scolded. "Who ever heard of an air camera?"

Teddy, who planned on being a famous director someday, didn't mind the teasing. "That's all right," he told her, shooting Bernie, then training his air camera on the rest of his friends. "When I'm living in Hollywood and making millions, I'll forgive you all. I may even use some of you as extras in my epics."

"Unless you can get famous by tomorrow," Nichole told him, her blue eyes flashing, "I'm not impressed." She folded her arms and pouted prettily. "We need the work right now."

"I'm afraid she's right," admitted Bernie. "If we want to keep going to the Friday night features at the Ridge Dale Cineplex or dropping by Pizza Paradise after school, we've got to start paying our own way."

"Don't forget our mall trips," Nichole reminded her. If there were a shopping championship, Nichole certainly would have made the national finals. "Fabulosa

8

is getting in some darling suede miniskirts next week," she announced.

"Sounds good to me," Teddy chimed in. "When do we go?"

Nichole ignored him. "I'll simply die if Sheila Forest gets one before I do!" Sheila was the snobbish daughter of a computer company executive, and one of the few girls in school who could outspend Nichole.

"It sounds like none of you is going to live too long if you don't get jobs," Roger laughed. "Boy, I'm glad my parents told me I don't have to work while I'm playing a sport. With practice every day, that could get rough."

"You jocks get all the breaks," Teddy complained. "Here I have to spend my formative years inhaling exhaust fumes in my dad's auto body shop." He winked at the girls. "Of course, working conditions would be a lot better if I had three shapely assistants."

"Ugh!" Nichole paled under her blush. "You mean crawl around filthy cars and get grease under my nails? I'd rather starve!"

"Well, then, it looks like we'll have to hit the streets again after school," Shelley announced. "Not that it will do any good," she added glumly. The three girls had spent all week going from one store and restaurant to another. But so far, in the entire town of Ridge Dale, New Jersey, not one business owner had any work for them.

"If we were old enough to drive, we could get jobs out of town," Bernie said. She sighed, thinking that even though the village of Ridge Dale was a friendly, picture-pretty town, the sort of place where people still waved to each other on the street, she sometimes wished

9

they lived in a big city. "I saw plenty of Help Wanted signs in the mall last weekend."

"I'm afraid the help they want isn't us," Shelley told her. "Unless your mom can drive us there whenever we need to work."

"With five children, my mom already has a full-time job," Bernie explained. She loved her big, busy family, but sometimes it seemed as though you needed name tags and a schedule to keep track of everyone!

When the bell rang for sixth period, all the students in the cafeteria struggled to their feet, picked up their trays, and formed a human wave that moved slowly toward the small conveyor belt at the back of the cafeteria. "Well, you two can comb the newspapers and go from store to store if you want," Nichole told her friends as a crowd of students closed in around them. "But I've made up my mind. "I'm going to work at Looking Good Boutique."

Bernie and Shelley stopped in their tracks. "But that's the most expensive, elegant store in town," Bernie said.

"All their staff are college students taking marketing courses," Shelley added.

"So what?" Nichole pushed ahead of them, slipping her tray onto the belt. "I don't just *study* fashion. I *live* it." She tossed her shining hair. "Besides," she added smiling her most photogenic smile, "I spend half my clothing allowance at Looking Good. Without me, they'd probably go out of business."

Teddy and Roger followed behind the girls, Teddy still at work with his imaginary camera. He elbowed his way through the crowd, fighting for room to film the girls. "I'm going to call this feature The Great Job Hunt," he announced, sighting them through his fingers.

"It'll be a movie that's got it all—gorgeous girls, cheap thrills, and the answer to the eternal question: Are women good for anything?"

Too late, Teddy ducked for cover as all three girls started raining napkins and straws on him. Laughing, he backed into Roger, who dropped all his silverware and half his leftover fries onto the floor. "Roger Thornton!" exclaimed Nichole, staring at the catsupy mess. "I don't know how anyone can be so coordinated on the football field, and so clumsy off it!"

As Roger blushed crimson and dropped to the floor on his knees, napkin in hand, his four friends forgot their squabble and helped him clean up. They had just finished when the second bell rang, and each of them had to hurry off to a different class. "Good luck this afternoon," Roger called after the girls. He waved good-bye to Teddy. Then, as soon as he'd put his tray away, he raced to catch up with Bernie, smiling shyly, walking her all the way to her class, even though he had to double back up three flights of stairs to his own.

2

"Bernadette O'Connor, Are You Out of Your Mind?"

"Here we are!" Nichole was her confident, breezy self outside Ridge Dale's most exclusive clothing store. Bernie and Shelley stared in awe at the elegant brick exterior, with its gold awnings and neon window displays. High above them, spelled out in glittering letters, were the words, Looking Good Boutique.

"Now you two stay here until I get my job," Nichole told her friends. "When I signal you to come in, I'll talk the manager into hiring you both." She handed Bernie her school books, grinning broadly. "I can't wait till the three of us are working together!" She checked her perfect features in the reflection of the plate glass window and disappeared inside.

Nichole had made it all sound so easy, so automatic,

that Bernie was surprised to see her friend coming back out the front door after only a few minutes. "Boy," said Shelley admiringly, "you must really spend a fortune in there to get hired so fast!"

But Nichole had lost her spark. She didn't look at them; instead, she walked a few steps from the store, then flounced down on the sidewalk. Bernie noticed she didn't even check to see if she would stain her powder blue skirt. Something was definitely wrong.

"It's not fair!" Nichole insisted. "After all the hideous clothes I've bought from that revolting store!" Her tone was fierce, but Bernie saw little tears of frustration under her mascaraed lashes.

"Revolting?" Shelley was confused. "But you love Looking Good. You always say they know what's in before New York does."

"What happened?" asked Bernie gently.

"She wouldn't hire me," Nichole whimpered. "That stuck-up Miss Dennis, the one who's always so nice to me when I shop there, she told me it's store policy not to hire anyone without experience."

"Experience?" Shelley could hardly believe it. "But you know more about clothes than anyone on the face of the planet!"

"I tried to tell her that," Nichole sniffed, smoothing the soft lap of her cashmere skirt. "But she wouldn't listen."

"How are we supposed to get experience," Bernie protested, "when no one will hire us without it?"

"Or find a job outside of town when we're too young to drive." Shelley sat down beside Nichole, her chin in her hands. She remembered how worried her dad's face had been, his stern warning about tightening their belts.

13

"And I thought high school was going to be different. But here we are, lowly freshmen, left out of everything."

"I read a book about a group of girls who made money by baby-sitting," offered Nichole. "I suppose if we only took well-behaved children, it wouldn't be too bad."

Bernie burst out laughing. "I can see you've never baby-sat before," she told her friend. "Take it from someone who has three younger sisters and a baby brother, you'd rather work on Teddy's dad's cars." Bernie had helped her mother take care of the younger children in her family ever since she was old enough to fasten diapers. "At least a car can't have an accident in your lap!

"Besides," she added thoughtfully, "wouldn't it be exciting to do something that really makes a difference, something important?"

"You mean like take a break from job-hunting to meet the gang at Pizza Paradise?" Nichole, who was feeling better already, stood up and turned her usual radiant smile on her two friends. "Haven't we suffered enough rejection for one day?"

Bernie laughed again and fell into step with the two other girls as they headed for their usual after-school hangout, a few blocks down the street. "I guess we have," she agreed, handing Nichole her books. "But I'm serious about making a difference. Why is everybody always talking about what we'll be when we grow up and telling us how we're going to change the world?" She shifted her backpack, her jade eyes taking on a determined shine. "I want to be someone right now. I want to change things right here."

14

"The only thing I want to change is this skirt," Nichole told them, as they reached the familiar white sign with the blue lettering and the cartoon drawing of a pizza slice with wings and a halo. "I've gotten a big smudge mark from moping around over that silly job." She brushed the back of her skirt with her hand. "If anyone special is in Pizza Paradise, I'll just die!"

"Well, then, get ready to die," Bernie whispered, as they walked in the door. "Because Brian Stone is sitting right over there with Roger."

"What?" Nichole gasped. She pulled her two friends back outside the door. "We're about to share a pizza with the hunkiest senior in the world, and you two aren't going to comb your hair?" She reached into her purse, fumbling through different shades of lipstick and tubes of eyeliner. "I thought Roger didn't even know Brian!"

"He does now," Shelley told her, staring through the glass window in the door. She laughed as Nichole made frantic fish faces in her compact mirror. "There is one little problem, though," she added, giggling.

"What do you mean?" Nichole asked, closing her lipstick.

"She means," Bernie told her, smiling in spite of herself, "Brian's with his girlfriend."

Sure enough. There were three people in the booth— Roger, Brian, and Mariah Tecknor. But stubborn Nichole wasn't used to giving up. "Her again," she said. "No prob." She straightened her skirt and pushed open the door. "I can outflirt a straight-A grind with one hand tied behind my back."

"Wait a minute!" Bernie and Shelley exchanged glances. When Nichole set her mind on something she couldn't have, there was usually trouble! They hurried

15

after their friend, but it was too late. By the time they reached Roger's table, Nichole was already slipping into the booth beside the two boys, chatting nonstop.

"I think football is positively the most fabulous sport in the world!" Nichole's voice was high and sugary; it didn't sound at all like the one she'd been using outside the restaurant a few seconds earlier. Mariah Tecknor smiled at Bernie and Shelley as they walked up, then made room on the seat beside her. Bernie felt at home with her right away.

"And of all the positions on the team," Nichole kept talking, turning to face Brian in the narrow booth, "I like fullback the best." She looked at the handsome, older boy as if no one else were with them. "Isn't that what you play, Brian?"

The senior shook his head. "No," he told her. "I play running back." He smiled politely, then turned to Roger. "I'm really glad to meet you, Thornton. And I think you're right. An end of season scrimmage with you guys is a great idea. Let's . . ."

"Well, they're both backs," Nichole interrupted him. "It's still football, isn't it?" She smiled winningly. "And if there's one thing I love, it's football."

"That's great," Brian said, with just a trace of annoyance. He turned back to Roger. "Maybe the captains should get together with the coaches and set up a date. How about . . ."

"That's the only reason I didn't go out for cheerleading," Nichole continued, interrupting again. "All the cheers are done facing the bleachers, and I decided I simply couldn't bear to miss a single play!"

Bernie could hardly believe her ears. She'd never heard Nichole even mention football or cheerleading.

16

(Unless you counted the time they'd passed Sheila Forest in the hall. Sheila had been wearing her cheerleading skirt and Nichole said it made her thighs look like 747's!)

"I didn't know you were such a football fan, Nichole," Roger said warmly. "Maybe you could help out with the stats at our frosh games."

"The what?" Nichole's lovely eyes looked vacant.

"The statistics. You could write them down in our score book. Coach says he really needs a hand."

Nichole blinked. "Well, I . . . I don't think so, Roger. I mean, no offense, but I'd rather work on the varsity games." She turned to Brian, her voice dropping to a whisper. "That is, I think I could be of more use there."

"Actually, I don't think so," Brian said. He reached across the table and took Mariah's hand. "We have a pretty special score keeper already." Mariah smiled back at him, and Nichole twisted uncomfortably in her seat.

"Mariah here knows the plays better than I do," Brian said proudly. "She's a real pro."

"I am kind of a nut when it comes to football," Mariah admitted now, smiling at Nichole. "Not many girls are, so I'm really glad I've got company." She patted Nichole's arm, her voice warm and sincere. "My dad was a college coach for years, and he has a classic collection of games on film. Maybe you could come over and we could watch them together sometime."

Nichole squirmed. "Maybe," she said. "But I'm going to be pretty busy from now on." At last she glanced at her two friends. "You see, the three of us are getting after-school jobs."

"Oh," said Mariah, "where are you working?"

17

"Actually," Bernie told her, glad of the chance to fit a word in, "we haven't found anything yet. It seems fourteen is too young for most jobs in town."

"Not for mine." Mariah, her friendly face framed by dark curls, grinned at Bernie.

"Really?" Shelley was interested now. "Where do you work, Mariah?"

"Mercy General."

"The hospital?" Bernie was confused. She remembered the huge stone building across town, the sound of ambulances streaking there in the middle of the night. "Are you a nurse?"

Mariah laughed. "No, I'm a J.V."

"A what?"

"A Junior Volunteer. Complete with uniform, bed-making callouses, and very sore feet!"

"Uniform?" Bernie had never seen Mariah in anything but casual school clothes. "What uniform?"

Mariah looked embarrassed. "I keep it in my locker and change after school so I won't get teased to death," she confessed. "Actually, it's kind of pretty—white with red pin stripes."

"Sounds like a fashion triumph," Nichole said. She stopped sulking long enough to give Mariah a broad, sarcastic smile. But the others ignored her. Bernie leaned forward eagerly. "So what does a J.V. do?" she asked.

"We help the nurses out," Mariah told her. "There's always more work than they can handle; we feed the patients, talk to them, get stretchers, even lend a hand in post-op."

"Post-op?" Bernie and Shelley looked at the older

18

girl, fascinated. Bernie hadn't dreamed any job for a teenager could be so important.

"That's short for postoperative," Mariah told them. "You know, when patients are recovering from operations. There's a lot to do then—letting families know the surgery's over, replacing oxygen masks, transporting patients back to their rooms." She smiled. "Sometimes I wish I had three hands!"

"Don't you wish you had a salary, too?" Nichole clearly hadn't forgiven Mariah for being Brian's girlfriend. "I mean being a J.V., that's just volunteer work." She sat stiffly in the booth, glaring at the older girl. "We're looking for *real* jobs."

Instead of being angry, though, Mariah just laughed. "You're certainly not the first person who's wondered why J.V.s work so hard for no money." She reached across the table, touching Nichole's arm again. "But all you have to do is see one little kid's face light up when you walk into the Pediatrics Unit. Or sit with one patient whose family forgot to visit. You'd know then that being a hospital volunteer is the realest job in town."

Shelley and Bernie were full of questions, and while the group finished the large pie Brian had ordered, everyone talked excitedly—everyone except Nichole, who half-listened while the others plied Mariah with questions about what it was like to work side by side with the nurses and doctors at Mercy.

"It's a lot of hard work," Mariah told them. "You have to go for training, and you don't get your certificate and your hospital pin until you've proven yourself."

"Certificate?" Shelley asked.

"Sure, there's a lot to learn before you can really help

19

out—everything from washing stretchers to handling lab specimens to scrubbing up.''

"Scrubbing up?''

"You know, putting on surgical gowns and masks.'' Mariah, who'd been working at Mercy ever since she was a freshman, smiled. "I remember how thrilled I was the first time I got to scrub up. Just like Doogie Howser!''

The others laughed. Except Nichole. It seemed as if she could hardly wait to leave. She sat slumped in her seat, staring at the flying pizza slices painted on the ceiling above their table. She hardly ate a bite or said another word. When it was time to leave, she stood up sighing and watched as Brian and Mariah walked off hand in hand. "Thank goodness,'' she said, as the freshman friends headed home. "I didn't think I could stand another minute of that girl's tacky perfume!''

Roger and the three girls followed Dale Avenue back to Looking Good, then turned off onto Farview Lane, gossiping and chatting until they reached Roger's house. "The coach should call practice early every day,'' he told them, grinning. "It's not too shabby to get walked home by three gorgeous girls!'' He waved and turned up his drive. "See you tomorrow.''

As the girls continued toward the Peters' mansion, Nichole was shocked to hear Bernie confide to them she'd found the job she wanted. "I've made up my mind,'' she announced, her green eyes shining. "I'm going to be a J.V.''

"Bernadette O'Connor, are you out of your mind?'' Nichole turned to her friend, hands on hips. "Do you mean to tell me for one minute you'd work and not get paid for it?'' She remembered the conversation in Pizza

Paradise. "Just because the girlfriend of some dumb jock has a bleeding heart."

"Dumb jock!" Shelley wasn't going to let Nichole off so easy. "A few minutes ago he was a major-league hunk."

"Well, looks aren't everything," Nichole told her friend sternly. "Besides, I don't want to spend my life memorizing disgusting football plays."

"And I don't want to spend my life waiting until I'm old enough to do something worthwhile," Bernie told her. "I'm serious about this, Nick." She stopped walking and faced her friends. "I hope you two will sign up for the training program with me."

Shelley looked apologetic. "Being a J.V. *does* sound pretty terrific, Bernie," she said. "But I really have to make money. Can you picture me telling Dad I've found a wonderful new job that pays absolutely nothing?"

"I'd like to earn some money, too," Bernie told her. She remembered how she'd had to sweet-talk her baby brother, Matt, into taking three dollars out of his plastic clown bank just so she could pay her science club dues last week. "But I think I'd rather make a difference."

"Well, *you* can work for nothing if you want to," Nichole told her, stopping beside the large wrought iron gate that marked the beginning of the Peters' driveway. "But I don't intend to waste my time." She waved good-bye and started off down the winding drive.

When Bernie and Shelley reached the O'Connors' roomy old victorian on Hill Crest Drive, Shelley turned down Bernie's invitation to come in for a coke. "I want to get home and grab the paper before Clarisse tears it to shreds," she explained. "I've got a lot of job hunting to do."

21

"That's okay," Bernie told her, smiling. "I'm getting used to being turned down."

"I hope you understand, Bernie." Shelley put a hand on her friend's shoulder. "I think working at Mercy sounds great, but I just have to find a job that pays. I owe it to my dad."

"I understand, Shell."

Bernie waved and headed up her porch steps, picking a roller skate and a teddy bear up off the next-to-the-top step. She dropped the roller skate into the toy box near the door, then carried the bear and her books inside. As she pushed open the front door, she was greeted with the whoops and yells of her two-and-a-half-year-old brother and his little friend from next door. The two toddlers came scooting across the hall like wind up toys, one blond, the other with red hair the same color as Bernie's.

She stooped down, stuffing the soft bear in the driver's seat of Mathew's plastic dump truck. "Hi, guys," she laughed, dodging as the truck took off, then circled back toward her ankles. She thought about the day, glad that she'd learned about the exciting work at Mercy.

Happy as she was, though, Bernie felt the tiniest twinge of disappointment. After all, she would have loved to sign up for the hospital's training with her two best friends. But it didn't really matter, she decided, drawn into the kitchen by the delicious smell of something sweet baking. Even if she had to do it alone, nothing was going to stop her from becoming a Junior Volunteer. Nothing.

3

"No, Doctor, Our Love Can Never Be!"

"Hmmmmm! Butterscotch brownies." Bernie opened the stove door, letting the heavenly smell fill the kitchen. "How did you know these were just what I needed?"

Mrs. O'Connor laughed. "For one thing, you're allergic to chocolate," she told her daughter. "And for another, you've been eating my butterscotch brownies since you were tall enough to reach over the table and sneak them off the plate!"

Bernie bent over the open stove, feeling the pleasant warmth. "How much longer?" she asked, staring impatiently at the pan of soft dough.

"Forever, if you don't shut the door." Mrs. O'Connor took a pretty blue serving plate from a cupboard. "About five minutes, if you do." She laughed again as the stove door slammed shut and Bernie looked at her watch.

"Does this mean you're not mad at me anymore?" Bernie asked, putting her books on the counter and taking a seat at the kitchen table.

"So our talk the other night actually registered?" Mrs. O'Connor smiled, her green eyes and dark auburn hair an older version of Bernie's. "I hope we weren't too hard on you, Honey. It's just that high school is something we'll all need to get used to." She touched one of the delicate gold studs in Bernie's ears. "Just like we'll have to get used to our daughter having pierced ears."

Bernie was glad she had parents who thought things over, parents she could talk to. "I'm really sorry I didn't ask you first, Mom." She remembered how she and Nichole had raced off to the Earring Emporium right after school. "It's just that I got so excited, I forgot."

"Well, it could be worse." Mrs. O'Connor smiled. "You could have gotten a nose ring! Besides," she added, "when you're ready to switch from studs, Grandma's pearl drop earrings are going to look terrific on you."

When she was little, Bernie used to ask her mother about the pair of beautiful earrings in her jewel box. "Those," Mrs. O'Connor had always told her, "are for grownups." Bernie could hardly believe they would soon be hers. "Thanks, Mom!" she exclaimed, standing up from the table and hugging her mother.

"In return, how about putting your books in your room and then rounding up the crew for a brownie party?" Mrs. O'Connor suggested. Bernie didn't have to be asked twice. In a flash, she'd retrieved her books and raced up the stairs.

A few minutes later, all the O'Connors minus one were seated around the big oak table, devouring brownies and tall glasses of milk. "Don't forget to save some for Dad," Bernie warned her sisters and brother. "You know how he sulks if he finds out we've polished them off without him."

"Right," agreed Tracy, a pretty ten year old with a bouncy red ponytail. "The only thing that makes him madder is watching Bernie's backhand." Mr. O'Connor, who had played tennis in college and who coached the JV tennis team at Ridge Dale, was always encouraging his girls to take to the courts. The younger ones loved it, but Bernie tried too hard and usually ended up swinging at air.

"I think Bernie plays great," insisted Sara, who was seven and had hair as red as her two older sisters. She smiled adoringly at Bernie. "I think she does everything great."

"Me, too," agreed Kelly, who at five years old always followed the leader.

Bernie laughed. "Thanks, girls," she said. "It's good to have my own personal cheering section in this bunch."

"I want to be just like you when I get old," added Kelly, eyes shining.

"You mean nine long years from now?" Mrs. O'Connor looked amused.

"Sorry, Kell," Bernie told her, smiling. "With that hair, you're not going to be like anybody in our family." She grinned at the only O'Connor without red hair. "I'm afraid with those green eyes and that dark hair,

25

you'll just have to settle for being a plain old movie star!''

Sara tousled her sister's jet black hair, and they all munched and chattered until Tracy pointed out that the brownies were gone. ''Not even a crumb left,'' she said, staring at the empty blue plate in the center of the table.

''Agghhhhhhhhhh!'' Suddenly Mathew's little friend from next door was red-faced and screaming. The family turned to find Mathew with both hands in Bobby's mouth. He was tugging furiously at the soggy half brownie Bobby was trying to swallow. ''Daddy bownie,'' he commanded in baby talk. ''Daddy bownie!''

Everyone laughed. Mrs. O'Connor explained that she didn't think their father would want a half-eaten brownie and promised to bake more. Finally, the three little girls went upstairs to finish a fort they were building in the playroom, and Bernie and Matt walked the sniffling Bobby home. When they got back, Bernie was glad to find her mother alone in the kitchen.

''There's something I'd like to ask you about,'' she said, slipping into a chair at the table, remembering the lonely feeling she'd had after school.

Mrs. O'Connor looked up from the sink, her voice sounded worried. ''What is it, Honey?'' she asked, then wiped her hands and took a seat opposite her daughter. Although she'd been a bank officer for years, Mary O'Connor had quit work when she was pregnant with Tracy. Bernie thought it must be boring to watch the kids all day, but right now she felt pretty lucky to have a stay-at-home mom who was there when you needed her.

''There's a job I'd really like to try for,'' she told her mother. ''But my friends won't take it seriously.''

She described the work Mariah did as a J.V. at Mercy. She told Mrs. O'Connor how much she wanted to do something important and useful. And finally, she confessed how unhappy she'd felt when Nichole had made fun of volunteers and Shelley had told her she needed a "real" job.

Her mother covered Bernie's hand with her own. "I think what you want to do is wonderful," she said. "And most of all, I think you have to follow your own instincts." She sat back, folding her arms and studying her pretty daughter. "You know I quit a job everyone called important for one most people thought didn't really matter at all." She smiled, and her blue eyes deepened. "And I've been doing the most exciting work in the world ever since."

Bernie reached across the table to hug her mother. "You're the best, Mom," she said.

"I'll second that!" Behind them, Frank O'Connor was smiling broadly. "Especially since I smell butterscotch." Bernie's father was a big, well-built man whose slightly gray hair made him look sophisticated, not old. He put his briefcase on the table, kissed his wife and daughter, then headed for the stove.

"Don't open that!" Bernie and her mother yelled in chorus. They looked at each other, laughing. Then Bernie went to the refrigerator for the milk, and Mrs. O'Connor lifted the newly washed blue plate out of the sink, wiping it dry and setting it once again in the middle of the table.

The next day Ridge Dale's cafeteria was as noisy and crowded as ever. Bernie was relieved to see her friends had saved her a seat at their usual table. "How can you look so happy?'' Teddy asked her, taking his notebook off the chair next to him. ''It's Friday, fish sticks with suicide sauce.''

''I could eat anything today,'' Bernie told him. ''I talked to Mariah Tecknor in Bio class this morning, and I've got great news.''

''It must be great if you can get *these* down.'' Nichole sniffed at a sauce-laden fish stick, then put it back on her plate. She was wearing a dark green sweater that set off her light hair. Her smiling, confident self again, she seemed to have put yesterday's futile job hunt and the disaster at Pizza Paradise completely behind her.

''I'll pass, too.'' Shelley frowned and gingerly picked the fish sticks off her plate, folding them into a napkin. ''I'll just save these for Clarisse.''

Bernie laughed. ''That dear old cat of yours is the best-fed pet in town,'' she said. ''What other kitty do you know that gets french pastries and rump roasts for dinner?''

Shelley put the wrapped fish sticks in her book bag. ''It's all those Home Ec cooking assignments,'' she explained. ''Dad doesn't get home until after I'm asleep, so I don't have anyone else to try them out on!''

Roger laughed. ''You can try them on me anytime, Shelley.'' He swallowed a forkful of fish sticks hungrily. ''My mom's on a diet, so we never have second helpings or desserts at our house.''

''So what's your good news, Bern?'' asked Nichole. ''And what could it possibly have to do with that boring Tecknor person?''

''Well, I told Mariah I'm really interested in working at Mercy,'' Bernie told them. ''And she gave me the name of the Director of Volunteers at Mercy. I'm going to call her today!''

Shelley frowned. ''Gee, Bernie,'' she told her friend. ''I sure wish I could sign up with you.''

''Sign up for what?'' asked Teddy.

''You can't be serious!'' As usual, Nichole ignored Teddy and turned to Bernie. ''You're still determined to work for free?''

''More than ever.'' Bernie smiled calmly, remembering what her mother had said about trusting your own instincts. ''I can't wait.''

''Can't wait for what?'' asked Teddy, still left out.

Now Roger, too, ignored the other boy. ''You mean you won't be going to Pizza Paradise anymore?'' He looked crestfallen. It was clear that coming to the hangout after practice to meet his friends was really important to him.

''Being a J.V. only means one or two days a week once training is over,'' Bernie told him, smiling reassuringly. ''You won't even miss me.''

''Want to bet?'' Roger stared back at her, perfectly serious. No wonder some of her friends had begun to tease Bernie about the crush he had on her!

''J.V.? What's a J.V.?'' Teddy, who had missed yesterday's discussion at Pizza Paradise, was very confused. ''Will someone please tell me what's going on?''

''Bernie wants to be a volunteer at the hospital,'' Shelley explained. ''You know, helping the nurses feed the patients, making beds, things like that.'' She looked apologetic. ''In fact, if I didn't have to make money, I'd like to be a J.V., too.''

''It only takes a few hours a week, Shell.'' Bernie

29

looked hopeful. "Maybe you could find a paying job the other days."

Shelley brightened. "Maybe so," she said thoughtfully. "It's not as if I've found anything else, anyway."

"And we wouldn't need to depend on anyone for rides," Bernie added. "The hospital's within walking distance."

Shelley smiled. "Sure," she said, "why not? At least till I find something else."

Bernie was delighted. "Great," she said. "I'll tell Mrs. Hurley to expect two more in the training class."

"Make that three," Nichole chimed in. She smiled sheepishly. "If you think for one minute I'm going to let my two best friends go off and make a zillion brownie points and have all sorts of adventures without me, you're crazy!"

Bernie felt like hugging her friends. If it hadn't meant standing up and knocking over a trayful of fish sticks, she would have. Shelley and Nichole hadn't let her down after all! Soon the three of them were busy planning for the class.

"It's supposed to start next week," Bernie told them. "So we'll have to sign up right after school."

"Just be sure and get back in time for our pig-out at the House of Wu," Roger told her.

"What?" Bernie was so excited about Mercy, she couldn't think of anything else.

"Tonight's the opening of *Revenge of the Preppies* at the cineplex," Teddy reminded her.

"Right," chimed in Roger. "And we all made plans to meet for Chinese before the show. Remember?"

Bernie knew they'd have to get to the theatre early. On opening nights, the line at the cineplex sometimes wrapped around the block. "Gee, Roger," she admitted. "I'm not sure how long it will take to sign up. Maybe you and Teddy should eat without us." She smiled at Roger. "Save me an egg roll, will you?"

"Boy," said Teddy. "This Florence Nightingale routine of yours could be a real bummer."

"Don't worry, Teddy." Shelley shook her head. "We don't intend to stop having fun."

But Teddy was already running a movie in his head. His face took on a dreamy expression and he turned to an invisible person beside him. "Yes, Doctor," he said in a high-pitched feminine voice. "Coming with the bedpan, Doctor."

"You are definitely deranged," Nichole told him, laughing in spite of herself.

Teddy, reveling in the attention, clasped his hands and sighed. "No, Doctor, our love can never be." He closed his eyes, pushing the air away. "I said no, Doctor. Our patients must come first."

"Let's leave this sicko to his soap opera and go make that call to Mercy," suggested Shelley. Even before the bell rang, the three girls stood up and took their lunch trays to the back of the room. As they waved to Teddy and Roger, Nichole couldn't resist teasing Bernie. "Roger is already missing you, Bern," she said. "He looks positively pathetic."

It was true. Roger still sat dejectedly at the table, looking as if he'd lost his best friend. "Oh, don't worry about him," Bernie reassured her friends, as they left the cafeteria and headed for the pay phone in the hall. "Once the boys see how exciting our work is, they'll want to sign up, too."

Bernie took the phone number Mariah had given her

31

out of her pocket and dialed. Meanwhile Nichole giggled beside her. "Can you imagine Teddy and Roger wearing nursing caps?"

The picture made Shelley laugh, too. She put her hands over her mouth as Bernie asked for the Volunteer Office. "It's a good thing boys can't be J.V.s," she whispered, "or the hospital would really be a mess."

Bernie, waiting to be connected, had heard her. "But they can," she explained. "Mariah says there are plenty of boys who work as junior volunteers."

"There are?" Nichole was taken by surprise. Suddenly she was much more enthusiastic about the program. "Tell them we can start today, Bern." She pushed her friend's shoulder, trying to reach the phone. "Tell them this afternoon will be just fine."

Bernie laughed, pulling the phone away. But her face turned serious when she heard Mrs. Hurley, Mercy's Director of Volunteers, on the other end of the line. She carefully explained why she'd called, then listened and nodded. Her two friends leaned closer, trying to hear the conversation. Bernie nodded again, then thanked Mrs. Hurley and hung up, smiling.

"She says there's a training class starting Monday that we can sign up for this afternoon." Bernie looked happy and flushed. "She says we'll need to spend three afternoons there next week, then if we go on Saturday, we'll have finished our training. Isn't it great?"

Shelley hugged her. "I can't believe we're really going to do it," she squealed.

"The class is small, just four girls and two boys," Bernie continued, her eyes shining. "Mrs. Hurley says we'll learn a lot faster that way."

"Two boys?" asked Nichole. "Did you say two boys?"

"She says we'll take a tour of every unit in the hospital on Monday," Bernie told them. "She says we can get our uniforms the next day."

"Two boys?" asked Nichole again.

Bernie laughed, pointing a finger at her boy-crazy friend. "Now, listen, Nick," she warned her, "remember what Teddy taught us."

"What?" Nichole looked puzzled. "What did that weirdo ever teach us?"

Bernie put her hand to her heart and said in the squeaky, high voice Teddy had used, "Our patients must come first."

Shelley and Bernie collapsed in laughter, and even Nichole had to smile. "Laugh if you want to," she told them. "But frankly I'm glad this job offers more than changing yucky beds and touching sick people." She shuddered at the thought. "Maybe Teddy the Terrible was right. Maybe being a volunteer will be romantic, after all!"

4

Nichole Gets the Jitters

Pat Hurley was a small woman with a ready smile and a halo of tight, silver curls. "I'm so glad to meet you," she told Bernie and her friends. She invited the three of them to sit down on the small couch and the leather chair in her office. "And I know a lot of patients who will be, too!

"You see," she explained, standing up and walking out from behind her desk, leaning against it in a friendly, easy way, "Mercy is a pretty big hospital; we draw patients from more than twenty towns in this part of New Jersey. Many families can't travel here to visit every day, so a cheerful face and a kind word from a young volunteer makes all the difference."

Bernie and Shelley smiled at each other, then at Mrs. Hurley. Nichole, though, didn't seem to have heard a word. She was staring intently at the bright floral pattern that covered the couch. "Did you have this upholstery done at Rapnick's?" she asked suddenly, running her hands over the fabric.

"I really don't know, dear," Mrs. Hurley told her. "Why?"

"My mother's having my whole bedroom redone," Nichole explained. "I love this pattern." She smiled broadly. "Wouldn't it make knock-out drapes?"

The Volunteer Director looked confused, and Shelley squirmed in her seat. Bernie, too, felt embarrassed. Why didn't Nichole ever think about anything but fashions and boys?

"Actually, you're right. That print *would* be pretty for curtains," Mrs. Hurley agreed cheerfully. "Now, if you girls still want to sign up, we have time for a tour of the hospital."

Nichole wore a worried expression her friends had never seen. "We don't have to actually go in any rooms, do we?" she asked. "I mean, we won't see any sick people?"

"I'm afraid we don't have time to talk with patients this afternoon," Mrs. Hurley said. "This will just be a quick look around."

"As long as it's quick," Nichole said, sounding very relieved. "We have a movie date."

"Well, this won't take long," Mrs. Hurley assured her. "You'll get the official tour on your first day of class next week." She picked up a clipboard and started out of the room. "I just thought you might like a sneak preview—including a soda at our snack shop."

"Sounds delicious," Bernie told her, then smiled, blushing. "I mean interesting," she corrected herself.

35

Mrs. Hurley laughed. "I hope it will be both," she said, and led them down the hospital corridor.

Bernie rushed home to eat and change for the movie that night. At the dinner table, she hardly ate a bite. She was too busy filling her family in on her exciting visit to Mercy. "You wouldn't believe how big it is," she said, recalling the impressive entrance, the carved lion above the door, one stone paw wrapped around a tiny lamb. "The buildings are set up like a compass, with a north, south, east and west wing."

"Gee," said Tracy. "All we've ever seen is the Emergency Room." She poked her little brother who was sitting next to her. "Every time Captain Crash here falls off his Fire Wheels."

"Rrrrummmm, rrrummmmm!" roared Matt, imitating a car engine, dribbling mashed potatoes from his mouth.

"Hey, Speed Demon," Mr. O'Connor cautioned. "Finish chewing before you take off."

"There are different units for different medical problems," Bernie went on excitedly. "We saw Orthopedics. That's where patients are recovering from fractures and broken bones." She talked away, while her food went untouched. "We saw the Long Term Care Unit—most of the patients there are elderly and need round-the-clock nursing."

Her face lit up suddenly. "Oh, and we saw Pediatrics today, too. All the nurses and doctors call it Peeds." She remembered Mrs. Hurley leading them from one brightly painted room to the next, from one tiny invalid to another. She remembered the little boy who was building a card house on his bed tray, the little dark-eyed girl clutching a stuffed kangaroo. "Those kids are

36

so cute and lively," she enthused, "you can hardly believe they're sick.

"And on Monday we'll see the rest of the units. I have to go to training classes Monday, Wednesday, and Friday after school." Bernie looked hesitantly at her mother. "And Saturday, too," she said. "Can we do the laundry on Sunday instead?" She knew her mother counted on her help with the family's huge weekend wash load.

Mrs. O'Connor nodded. "I won't mind putting off that chore any more than you will," she said, grinning.

"Can I be a J.V., too?" asked Sara, wide-eyed.

"Me, too," chimed in Kelly. "I want to help the nurses."

"Sorry, guys," Bernie told her sisters. "You're not old enough." She felt kind of proud. "You have to be fourteen."

"Why?" asked Kelly. It was one of her favorite questions.

"Well, because the hospital needs to make sure you're serious," Bernie told her. "They figure a freshman in high school won't let them down." She remembered how Nichole had worried about missing the movie, the way she'd sulked through the tour, looking angry and bored. "I sure hope they're right," she added.

"What do you mean?" Bernie's father had caught the anxious tone in his eldest daughter's voice.

"It's Nichole," she confessed. "I don't think she really wants to be a volunteer. She couldn't wait to get out of there today."

"Give her time," Mr. O'Connor told Bernie. "Nichole might come through when it counts."

37

"Then she better come through fast," said Bernie. "Training starts in two days, and that's when it counts."

But on Monday afternoon, when the three friends walked to Mercy after school, Nichole was wearing the same nervous expression Bernie had noticed during the interview with Mrs. Hurley. "I hope we don't have to talk to any patients right away," she said, as they turned down the long driveway to the hospital's Volunteer Office. "Sick people give me the creeps."

In the reception area outside the office, three other teenagers were waiting, sitting expectantly in chairs around a large formica conference table. There was a tall girl who kept crossing and uncrossing her long legs. There was a good-looking black boy with a varsity letter on his wrestling jacket. And there was a short blond boy who wore glasses and buried his face in a magazine.

Nichole sized up the group. "Two nerds and a jock," she whispered as the three friends walked in. Seeming more like her old self, she headed for the empty seat between the wrestler and the girl, while Shelley and Bernie took seats beside the boy absorbed in *Newsweek*. They all looked at each other, but no one spoke.

Finally, the tall, nervous girl broke the silence. She grinned at the others, then said to no one in particular, "I hate waiting, don't you?"

Bernie was glad to have a chance to get to know the others. "Me, too," she told the girl. "My name's Bernadette." She smiled reassuringly. "These are my friends, Shelley and Nichole. We go to Ridge Dale. Where are you from?"

The girl had a narrow face and wore her hair parted down the middle, accentuating her thin, bony look. "I'm

Julie Hayden, I'm a freshman at East Wood," she told Bernie. "Nice to meet you, Bernadette."

"It's really Bernie," Bernie laughed. "Bernadette's a bit much." She turned to the two boys. Both of them were watching the girls, the blond boy peering at them over his copy of *Newsweek*. "How about you?" she asked. "Where do you go to school?"

The reader rolled his magazine up and put it in his lap. "I'm from Hayward High," he told them. He looked across the table at the wrestler. "So's Willard." He blushed for a moment. "Of course, it's a big school. We don't really know each other very well."

The handsome black boy looked confidently around the table. "Hi," he said. "I'm Blake Willard." He grinned at the blond boy. "My friend here, who forgot to introduce himself, is Clifford Foster. He's Hayward High's ace debater."

Clifford blushed again, the color spreading from his neck all the way up to the roots of his pale hair. "It's just Cliff," he said. He glanced hesitantly at the other boy. "I'm honored, Blake. I didn't think varsity letter-men like you even knew debate existed."

"Hey, Cliff," Blake told him, "I hear you've really racked up some speaker points. My dad debated in college, and he says it takes lightning-quick thinking."

Bernie smiled at Blake. She liked the way he took time to make Cliff feel good about himself. She could see he'd be great with patients.

Nichole, on the other hand, clearly wasn't thinking about patients right now. "Speaking of lightning-quick," she said to Blake, "I'll bet it takes terrific re-flexes to be a wrestler." She was using her soft, flirty

39

voice, staring at Blake's jacket. "I just love to watch wrestling. It's my favorite sport."

Bernie and Shelley exchanged glances. "Gee, Nichole," said Shelley, who couldn't resist teasing, "you sure have a lot of favorite sports."

Nichole gave her friend an injured look, then turned back to Blake. "Are you Hayward's captain, Blake?"

Clifford interrupted. "You bet he is!" he told Nichole. "In two sports. This is Mr. Jock, you're talking to."

Nichole barely looked at Clifford. "That's wonderful," she purred, turning again to Blake. "What's your other sport, baseball?"

Blake smiled. "No," he said. "I play football right now. Baseball and wrestling are both spring sports."

"She knew that," Shelley giggled. "She was just testing you. Right, Nichole?"

For once, Nichole took things in good humor. She smiled broadly, her blue eyes flashing like a cover girl's. "Okay," she admitted. "Maybe I'm no expert on sports." She looked around the table, winning everyone's hearts without trying. "But I'd love to learn."

"Deal," said Blake, smiling back. "Maybe you could all come to one of our matches."

Bernie remembered how Roger had told them he couldn't take a job during the season. "What about football practice, Blake?" she asked their new friend. "How can you be a J.V. and a team captain at the same time?"

"The training's only one weekend," Blake told them. "I arranged that with the coach before the season started. And then I asked Mrs. Hurley for special evening hours, so I can work here after practice."

"Wow!" Julie seemed more relaxed now, her nose

40

crinkling as she laughed. "You're going to be one tired puppy at night."

Blake smiled back at her. "Well, let's just say I won't have much trouble falling asleep," he said.

The entire group was chatting like old friends when Mrs. Hurley walked into the room. "Well," she told them, "I see you've gotten to know each other." They quieted now, and made a place for her at one end of the table. "That's good," she said, smiling as she sat between Julie and Shelley. "Because there won't be a whole lot of time for talking once we get started."

She looked at the group, sounding a bit more serious now. "You see, when you're on duty in one of our units, you'll be expected to give all your attention to our patients." She folded her arms, leaning against the formica table top, studying each of their faces in turn. "I'm not being dramatic when I say that what you bring to Mercy is very, very important. And we need you to give one hundred percent."

Bernie and Blake nodded, but nobody spoke. Mrs. Hurley went on. "Don't worry, though," she said, smiling again, "there'll always be a nurse to help you, to set you back on track if you take a wrong turn." She gathered a clipboard and some papers from in front of her and started passing pages around the table. "And, believe me, everybody makes mistakes at first. It's part of learning."

Each youngster at the table got two pieces of paper, one labeled *Do's and Don'ts for Mercy Volunteers*, the other headed *Junior Volunteer Fall Schedule*. Bernie saw that the schedule left blanks to be filled in, spaces where she could choose what days and hours she wanted to work at the hospital. There was a space for every

41

day of the week after school and for both days of the weekend. Bernie was so thrilled to finally be here, to be starting training at last, she wanted to fill in every blank!

"Now, don't rush into a commitment," Mrs. Hurley advised, as if she had read Bernie's mind. "Keep this material and go over it at home with your parents. You have three more days of training, and after that you'll have a much better idea of what a Mercy Volunteer does.

"So why don't we get started?" As she stood up from the table, the six eager students stood up with her, whispering excitedly to each other as they followed her out of the Volunteer Office and down the hall. Hurrying along with the rest, Bernie could hardly believe that in just one more day, they'd be walking down these same halls in uniform!

"I don't need to tell you what unit this is," said Mrs. Hurley as she stopped, then gathered the group in front of a glass wall that separated them from a roomful of basinettes, each filled with a tiny, red-faced baby. "The risk of infection to a newborn is pretty high, so you won't usually be assigned to the Nursery." She paused, putting a finger up to the glass as if she could soothe a small, dark-haired baby who was crying heartily, clenching its fists and rolling its head from side to side. "I just like to show off my favorite patients!"

Most of the boys and girls pressed against the glass, oohing and aahing, trying to get the attention of one of the babies. "Aren't they just precious?" asked Julie, making a kissing mouth in the direction of a basinette where twins lay sleeping, a pink hospital band around each of their tiny wrists.

But Nichole was not impressed. She shrank back from the glass. She looked at the rows of squirming infants and shuddered. "Imagine changing all those diapers!" she said with disgust.

Bernie hoped that something on their first-day tour would catch Nichole's interest, but it was the same with every place they visited. In the Day Accomodation Room, where patients were recovering from minor surgery, Nichole ran off when she saw the black stitches (Mrs. Hurley called them "sutures") in an old man's cheek. The man looked up in surprise when the pretty teenager put her hand over her mouth. "It doesn't hurt," he tried to assure her, but Nichole had already turned her back on the group and disappeared.

When they visited the Dietary Department, things didn't go any better. Mrs. Hurley showed the new trainees the menu blanks they would pick up and distribute to patients in their units. But Nichole hardly listened, and she refused to touch one of the trays that had been brought back from a patient's room. "It might have germs on it," she told Mrs. Hurley, looking as pathetic and queasy as if she'd already caught some horrible disease.

Even the Transport Department didn't lift her spirits. While the other boys and girls eagerly practiced the correct procedures for preparing stretchers and for moving and braking wheelchairs, Nichole stood off to one side, not participating at all. She stared at the others, a defiant, snobbish expression on her face. Bernie knew that look. Her friend was afraid.

"What is it, Nick?" she asked quietly, when they had left Transport and were on their way back to the Volunteer Office. "What's wrong?"

43

Nichole didn't look at Bernie. She walked straight ahead down the hall, her eyes on her own neat black pumps. "I'm not cut out to be a J.V., Bernie." Her voice shook. "I'm not like you and Shelley. I'm just not."

"What do you mean?" asked Bernie. "Mrs. Hurley says everyone gets the jitters at first."

"Not like me," Nichole insisted. "Ever since I was a little girl I hated being sick."

Bernie laughed. "I don't think anybody likes it," she said kindly. "That's only natural."

"No, it's different with me." Nichole's voice dropped to a whisper. Finally, she stopped in the middle of the hall and turned to face her friend. "You don't understand, Bernie. I'm scared. I'm really scared. I hate being around sick people. I thought I was going to throw up when I saw that man's stitches." She shook her blond head. "I'll never make it here."

Bernie had never seen her cool, confident friend so upset. She stared down the hall at the group of laughing boys and girls, all of them looking forward to the next day of training. Maybe Nichole was right. Maybe she just wasn't meant to be a volunteer. Still, one day wasn't enough to find out. "You'll be fine, Nick," she insisted, looping an arm through her friend's. "You wait and see."

"They won't even let you wear earrings," Nichole complained.

"See, you've already learned the Do's and Don'ts," laughed Bernie. "You're way ahead of me, Nick."

"Or colored nail polish," wailed her friend.

"I'm telling you, Nichole, by the end of training you'll be a whiz." Bernie sounded breezy and casual,

44

but she wasn't really so confident. What if Nichole didn't get through the training program? What if she couldn't earn her certificate? As she and Nichole joined the others in the office, Bernie wasn't at all certain what the rest of the week held in store. But she knew one thing for sure. She wasn't about to let her friend give up on herself yet!

5

Roger Gets the Blues

The new volunteers had no training class the next day. Even so, Mercy was all Bernie could think about. "I can't wait until tomorrow," she told her friends over a deluxe pie at Pizza Paradise after school. Her excitement was contagious. The other girls at the table leaned forward, eager to hear more. All of the other girls, that is, except one.

Nichole rolled her china-blue eyes. "Honestly, Bernie," she said. "I don't know why you're making such a big deal out of being a J.V. It's not like we're nurses or anything."

"Are you kidding?" Shelley sounded every bit as enthusiastic as Bernie. "Training at Mercy is absolutely the most thrilling thing I've ever done. Besides," she added, looking proudly around the table, "Mrs. Hurley says without us, the nurses couldn't do their job."

Elise Sheridan and Beverly Feldon listened wide-eyed. Elise, a stout, friendly girl who sat beside Shelley, nodded. "That's what my parents tell me about my helping out in our bakery every day after school." She looked at the others, then giggled. "Of course, the only thing exciting about *my* job is the jelly doughnuts!"

"Don't forget your salary," said Nichole, picking the pepperoni off her slice of deluxe. "At least you're earning money for the work you do. The only thanks we get for wearing ridiculous uniforms and exposing ourselves to hideous germs is a sweet smile."

"Uniforms?" asked Beverly, who sat between Nichole and Bernie. "Do you get to choose the color?" A majorette for Ridge Dale's marching band, Beverly loved the short-skirted, blue and white uniform the twirlers wore.

"Oh, Bev, you should come with us. You'd make a great volunteer!" Shelley smiled at the thought. Wouldn't it be terrific if all their friends worked at Mercy!

But Bev was a teenage dynamo who belonged to more clubs and was into more activities than she could keep track of. "Gee," she told Shelley, "I wish I could." She thought for a minute, staring at the winged pizzas painted on the ceiling, running through her busy schedule. "No," she said at last. "I've got something to do every single day after school." She looked at the others apologetically. "Weekends, too," she sighed.

"Well," announced Nichole, "you're not missing much." She wished her friends would stop telling the world about Mercy. She dreaded going back to the hospital tomorrow, but she buried her fear under a mountain of complaints. "We don't get to choose the color of our

47

uniforms. We can't shorten the hems or even add colored stockings. It's enough to turn your stomach."

"Then you won't be wanting seconds, will you?" Teddy Hollins stood smiling down at the five girls, waiting for an invitation to join them. Bernie shoved Nichole until she grudgingly made room for one more. "Roger's coming, too," Teddy announced as he helped himself to a slice of the pie. "The coach kept him after practice today."

"Gee, nothing's wrong, is it?" asked Bernie.

"Nope," Teddy told her in between bites. "Just some chalk talk for the big game against Hayward."

"We play Hayward?" asked Nichole, suddenly interested. "One of the J.V.'s is on the Hayward team." She remembered Blake's friendly smile and felt just a little bit better about having to face Mercy again.

"Wait a minute, there," said Roger Thornton, who joined them, laughing. "Don't tell me someone studying to be a nurse plays football!" He sat down beside Shelley and Elise, reaching across the table for the last slice of pie.

Bernie turned to Roger. "I've tried to tell you, Rog. The work at Mercy isn't just for girls. In fact, two of the J.V.'s in our training class are guys."

"And in less than two weekends, one of them is going to be playing against the varsity." Shelley told him, grinning.

"In fact," added Nichole, sounding important, "he's Hayward's captain."

"Doctor, Doctor!" Now Teddy assumed the high, whiny voice he used to make fun of the volunteers. "Have you seen my football?"

"Oh-oh." Roger was joining in the joke. He picked

48

up his notebook and stuffed it under the tablecloth. He spoke to Teddy in deep, rumbling tones. "I'm sorry, Nurse. But I seem to have sewn it up in this patient."

Teddy looked down in horror at the lump in the white cloth. Then he grabbed a table knife and handed it to Roger. "Here's your scalpel, Doctor," he said in his high-pitched voice. "You'll have to operate quickly if I'm going to make the second half."

Bev couldn't help smiling. "You two are terrible," she said, shaking her head. "I just hope you're still laughing after the Hayward game." Then she turned back to the girls. "Go on, tell us more about Mercy. I think it sounds awesome, just like General Hospital!"

"Well, it might not be all that dramatic," Bernie told her. "But it sure makes you feel good." She remembered the lonely older patients in the Long Term Care Unit, the way their faces had lit up when the young trainees walked into their rooms.

But Nichole had different memories. "Mrs. Hurley made me take all my bracelets off," she said, frowning. "And there are people there with open cuts and horrible tubes down their throats." She shuddered. "It's like working in Frankenstein's lab!"

"Speaking of horror shows," interrupted Roger, "I hope you guys aren't going to hold last week's game against me." He winked at Bernie. "I know we got kicked around pretty badly, but I can promise you a better performance this Saturday. We're playing a team that hasn't won a game all season!"

"No can do, Roger," Shelley told him. "This weekend is when we finish our training."

Bernie looked at Roger apologetically. "I'm afraid that's right, Rog," she said. "Saturday we get our cer-

49

tificates!'' She flushed with enthusiasm, her green eyes sparkling. She couldn't help showing how proud she was.

"You mean you'll miss my game?'' Roger sounded a little surprised and a lot disappointed. "But the gang's been to every game this season.''

"I'm really sorry.'' Bernie knew Roger counted on having his friends in the stands. "Maybe we can all get together Saturday night.''

"Not me,'' Roger told her. "Saturday's my dad's birthday. The whole family's going out to dinner.''

"Well,'' Teddy announced, not in the least upset, "I guess it's my duty to escort these lovely, lonely women all by myself.''

Bernie hoped Roger understood. "We just can't miss training,'' she explained. "We have to show Mrs. Hurley we're dependable.''

"Well, I'm glad *someone* can depend on you,'' said Roger, his eyes suddenly angry under his lowered brows. "I just wish your friends could.''

"Hey, old man,'' Teddy told him. "Aren't you being a little rough?'' He looked at Roger and shrugged his shoulders. "I mean, it's just one game, right?''

But Roger didn't answer. He looked at Bernie and the others, then glanced across the room to another table. "Excuse me,'' he said, waving to a group of football players who sat with Brian Stone. "I'd rather play football than doctor.'' He stood up, smiled stiffly at his friends, then headed toward Brian's table. "See ya,'' he said.

Teddy and the girls watched him walk away. They could hardly believe the way their normally easy-going friend had acted. "Boy!'' said Elise, breaking the awkward silence at last. "For a good football player, he sure is a bad sport!"

"Oh, he's okay," Teddy assured her. "He's just got a bad case of the Bernie blues."

"The what?" Elise put down her pizza and stared at her fellow freshmen. Everyone else at the table turned to look at Bernie, who felt a blush spread across her face.

"Where have you been, Elise Sheridan?" asked Nichole, grinning broadly. "Allow me to fill you in." She leaned forward, speaking in a whisper the whole table could hear. "You see, Roger has a giant, big-screen crush on our Bernie here." She smiled at her friend. "That's why he's not too crazy about her being a volunteer instead of a football fan."

"Come on, Nick," begged Bernie. "You turn everything into romance." She hoped that Roger was just worried about Hayward, that things would get back to normal after the big game. "He's got a lot on his mind."

"Is that why he keeps looking over here with that tragic puppy face?" Nichole was right. Roger's mind certainly didn't seem to be on the conversation he was having with Brian and the other players. Every few words, he glanced back at Bernie's table with a troubled expression, like someone who wanted to apologize but couldn't.

Suddenly, Bernie felt discouraged. The excitement and anticipation she'd felt about tomorrow had disappeared. Was being a J.V. going to cost her Roger's friendship? Had she made a mistake by asking Nichole to give Mercy a try? How had everything gotten so complicated, anyway? "I think I'll head home," she

51

said softly, standing and gathering up her books. "I've got some math problems with my name on them."

Bernie had even bigger doubts about Nichole the next day when Mrs. Hurley handed out the uniforms they'd ordered. First, Nichole complained that her pretty red-striped tunic was the wrong size. Then, she refused to wear her name tag, insisting that the pin would damage the fabric.

As for the rest of the trainees, they couldn't have been happier. "I can't believe it!" said Julie, studying her reflection in the mirror outside the reception room. She looked crisp and fresh, her long hair pulled back with a clip, her new white shoes as clean as the white stripes in her uniform.

Shelley took her turn in front of the glass, twirling from side to side to see the pretty way the tunic flared. "Oh," she thought. "Is this really me?"

Blake and Cliff, who wore maroon blazers with light trousers, also checked themselves out in the mirror. They caught each other stealing glances at the glass, high-fived, and laughed. "My man!" Blake told his new friend. "You're looking good!" Cliff, his pale hair slicked back behind his large ears, blushed redder than ever.

"These uniforms are yours, of course," Mrs. Hurley told them. "But they reflect on Mercy, so I want you to make sure they're spanking clean each time you report for duty."

Bernie was so full, so excited, she could hardly speak. It was hard to recognize Bernadette O'Connor in the smart, professional looking figure she saw in the glass. She studied the striped uniform, the name card with the letters that spelled her name backwards. *This is the beginning,* she thought to herself. *This is the start of something real and important. Isn't it strange to know that now? To see my life changing in a mirror?*

But they didn't have long to admire themselves. The second day of training was just as full as the first. They visited Central Supplies, learned about requisition forms and how to place orders for different units. They studied the way to change water carafes, how to label and deliver them on water carts to every room in a unit. The trainees listened attentively while Mrs. Hurley, then the floor nurse in Pediatrics, explained the procedures. Everyone was focused, straining to learn.

Everyone except Nichole, that is. "Big deal," she whispered. "Why all the fuss about water?"

The floor nurse heard her. "Because, young lady," she said firmly, "some patients' charts are marked NPO." She looked at the group. "That stands for a Latin phrase, and it means "Nothing by mouth." Now she directed her glance only at Nichole. "That means the patient should not have anything, even fluids. To give them water by mistake could slow their recovery or . . ." she paused, "or worse."

By the end of the day, Bernie and Shelley were dizzy with what they'd learned. On the walk home, they recited the names of the hospital's units, the procedures for infection control, what to do in a Code 9 patient emergency or a Code 12 area disaster.

As the two girls talked, they entirely forgot Nichole, who walked beside them, quiet and discouraged. At the driveway of the Peters' mansion, the pair stopped their discussion long enough to say good-bye. "See you tomorrow, Nick!" they called out, resuming their animated chatter without noticing how strangely silent their bubbly friend had turned. Neither of them looked back to see that Nichole hadn't made her way up the drive, but was standing instead by her gate, watching them as they walked off together.

Bernie could hardly wait until Friday. Thursday seemed to crawl by, especially since Roger was doing his best to make her choose between him and Mercy. At lunch, he carried his tray to the table where Bernie and her friends were already drowning the taste of Thursday's special with mountains of catsup.

"Mind if I join you?" he asked cheerfully, swinging one long leg over a chair. Then he stopped, the tray still in his hands. "Or is this going to be all hospital talk?"

Bernie tried to be patient. "How about we give football equal time?" she proposed, smiling up at him.

"Fine," he agreed, sitting beside her, reaching for the catsup. "I'll just leave when we get to the hospital part."

"I'll go with you," Nichole decided. She pushed her tray aside with one carefully manicured hand. "If I have to listen to Shelley and Bernie talk about wonderful Mrs. Hurley or sacred Mercy anymore, I'm going to lose my lunch."

Shelley and Bernie looked at each other. "Okay," said Shelley, grinning slyly. "Bernie and I won't talk about Mercy, Nichole, if you won't talk about clothes."

"Well, that's just ridiculous!" retorted their friend. She looked as though Shelley had suggested she go on a starvation diet. "Clothes are *crucial*!"

Everyone laughed, and for a while at least, they relaxed. But the next afternoon, when Nichole didn't meet

Bernie and Shelley at three o'clock by the big stone bench outside Ridge Dale's gym, Bernie was worried. "Maybe Nichole's decided not to go for training anymore," she told Shelley. "I guess being a J.V. isn't for everyone."

"But Nichole wanted to work at Mercy," Shelley said. "At first, that is." She remembered the way their friend had joked about every step in the training, the way she'd interrupted and talked through all Mrs. Hurley's instructions. She glanced at her wristwatch. "It's awfully late. Do you think we should leave without her?"

Bernie didn't want to miss any of the training. But she didn't want to give up on Nichole, either. "Maybe we could leave her a note," she suggested. "We'll stick it in the bench."

The two friends were busy writing when Nichole walked up behind them. "Is that a love letter to Roger?" she asked, teasing.

"Where have you been?" asked Shelley turning around, relieved. "We thought you weren't coming."

"Not coming?" Nichole laughed uncertainly. "I told you before, I wasn't going to let my two best friends have adventures without me."

But Bernie heard how nervous Nichole's laugh was, how thin and high her voice sounded. "Are you okay?" she asked, still worried.

"Of course, I'm okay," Nichole insisted. "Now let's get going. We don't want to be late for Mother Hurley." She raced off ahead of them, forcing her two confused friends to chase after her.

By the time they got to Mercy, the rest of the J.V.'s were getting ready to visit the Post Anesthesia Care

Unit, the PAC that Mariah had told them about. "You're just in time," Mrs. Hurley announced, smiling at the panting trio. "Today's the day we play doctor!"

What she meant was that before they entered the room where patients recovered from surgery, the volunteers had to put on green surgical gowns, rubber gloves, and masks. While the others rushed to the nurses' lounge to change into the special garb, Nichole hung back. She was the last one to dress and the last one to follow the group into the Recovery Room.

The nurse in charge of the Recovery Room met them just inside the entrance. She led them through the area, and they watched with excitement while orderlies wheeled in anesthetized patients. Everyone listened carefully as the nurse explained how to enter patients' names in the Recovery Room log, how to call the desk when patients were returned to their rooms, how to help the nurses with stretchers and oxygen masks.

But one volunteer hardly heard a word. Nichole was strangely quiet, as dazed and still as if she were one of the groggy patients. She barely moved, her eyes wide, her mouth set. When she left the Recovery Room to change clothes with the others, she walked with an awkward gait, her legs rigid, locked at the knees. Finally, when they had reached the hall, she hung behind, bracing herself against a door.

"What's the matter, dear?" Mrs. Hurley asked. "Are you all right?" Gently, the little woman approached Nichole and took off her mask. The trainees gasped with surprise. The pretty girl's face was pale with fright, huge tears hung in the corners of her eyes. "Let's get you some water," Mrs. Hurley said in a calm, reassuring voice.

Nichole nodded, and Blake scampered to a water cooler down the hall. He brought back a paper cup and handed it to the Volunteer Director. Mrs. Hurley thanked him, then put her arm around Nichole and walked with her down the hall, away from the others. Bernie held her breath as the two walked off. *Oh, no!* she thought. *Mrs. Hurley is going to tell Nichole she's out of the program. She'll be so embarrassed. Why did I ever drag her into this?*

At the end of the session, though, Nichole walked home with Shelley and Bernie as usual. She acted as though nothing at all had happened, and her friends were too considerate to mention her talk with Mrs. Hurley. Instead, the three of them chatted about school and clothes and the game with Hayward. When they got to Nichole's gate, she waved as usual, smiling like her old self. "See you tomorrow," she called. "That's when we get our certificates!"

Bernie and Shelley were curious. What had happened between Mrs. Hurley and Nichole? Why was Nichole coming back? Try as they might, they couldn't figure it out. And they knew they'd have to wait for the answers until Saturday afternoon, when the J.V.'s met for their last training class.

6

Nichole Comes Through

Nichole looked frightened when she arrived at Mercy the next day. Frightened but determined. There was a new set to her jaw, a steeliness in her blue eyes, a look that said, This is not easy, but I'm going to do it. She stood in the group with the others, listening carefully to everything Mrs. Hurley told them. "Today's your last day of training," the Volunteer Director said, smiling. "So I've saved the most important lesson for the end." She started off down the hall, the volunteers following proudly in their new uniforms. "First stop," Mrs. Hurley called over her shoulder, "the Flower Room!"

The Flower Room was small, packed with hospital carts and countless flower arrangements freshly delivered that morning from Ridge Dale Florists. The blooms filled the room with their perfume and color, bending this way and that from baskets and vases and little ceramic planters. "Ohhhh!" said Nichole softly when she saw them. "How lovely!"

The class watched while Mrs. Hurley showed them how to check off the deliveries on a list, how to arrange the flowers by room number and unit on the carts. "Now," she told the trainees, pushing one of the carts toward an elevator in the hall, "we're ready to make someone very happy."

The elevator stopped at the Long Term Care Unit on the third floor. The J.V.'s filed off and followed Mrs. Hurley to a room at the end of the floor. Mrs. Hurley lifted a basket of carnations and baby's breath off the cart, handing it to Bernie. "This goes to the window bed. The patient's name is Hilda Mallory. Why don't we go in and say hello?"

Bernie had learned to take the green clipboard with her, to say hello and ask the patient to sign a receipt for the flowers. What she hadn't learned was how to deal with a patient like Mrs. Mallory!

The old woman with the wispy gray hair sat drawn into herself. When the visitors said hello, she didn't answer. When Bernie held out the pretty basket, she stared through the flowers as if they weren't even there. In contrast to other patients who had been glad to see the young visitors, Hilda Mallory glared at the volunteers as though they were intruders, pulled her sheets around her, then turned her face to the window.

Bernie was baffled. "Would you like me to read you the card?" she asked gently. "Don't you want to know who these lovely flowers are from?"

Mrs. Mallory didn't turn around. "I know who they're from," she snapped. "I already know. Just put them with the others."

Sure enough, there were three other arrangements stretched along the top of a dresser on one side of the room. Julie stepped forward, trying to be helpful. "Gee," she told Mrs. Mallory with a friendly smile. "Somebody sure wants you to get well fast!"

The old woman turned her watery eyes toward Julie. "First of all, young woman," she said, "I'm not going to get well. And second, those flowers just mean my daughter doesn't have to visit."

Julie swallowed hard, then stepped back with the others. "Sorry," she said, so quietly that no one heard her.

"Well, you've got lots of visitors right now," Blake told Mrs. Mallory. His ready smile and charm had won over most of the patients the volunteers had seen during their training. Everyone seemed to feel better around Blake. "In fact," he added, "I'll bet you have more people in your room right now than any other patient on the floor!"

Mrs. Mallory didn't return Blake's smile. Instead, she shook her head irritably and waved him away. "The last thing I need is a troop of strangers around my sick bed," she said. "So just put those flowers down and leave me alone."

Bernie, who still stood by the bed with the floral arrangement, didn't know what to do. She looked back at Mrs. Hurley, but the Volunteer Director seemed as confused as her charges. She shrugged and nodded at Bernie, who walked to the dresser and put down the basket.

"Wait!" Nichole put her arm on Bernie's. "I've got an idea." She looked around the room, then walked to Mrs. Mallory's side. "Excuse me, Ma'am," she said.

60

"But I think you're right. The last thing this room needs is another basket of flowers."

Mrs. Mallory turned in bed to look at Nichole. "I mean it's just too tacky, isn't it?" the pretty J.V. asked. "What you need is something that makes a fashion statement. Something with flair."

Mrs. Mallory and the others watched in amazement as Nichole started pulling the flowers from their basket. "Let's see," she said to herself, tearing out a handful of baby's breath, "we'll need a few of these." She grabbed a fistful of carnations now, sitting in the chair beside Mrs. Mallory's bed, her head bent over the flowers in her lap.

"What on earth are you doing, child?" Mrs. Mallory's curiosity had gotten the better of her, and she sat up in bed, trying to see what Nichole was up to.

"There, that's better," Nichole announced finally, smiling. "Now, all we need is a safety pin. Has anyone got one?"

The volunteers and Mrs. Hurley looked helplessly around the room, but Mrs. Mallory knew what to do. "In my purse," she told Nichole. "Over there, on the dresser."

Nichole handed her the purse, then fished some fat green leaves out of the basket while Mrs. Mallory found a safety pin. A few more seconds, and Nichole was finished. "Now *that*," she said, holding up her creation proudly, "has style."

Everyone sighed with delight. Nichole's sense of color and design had worked a minor miracle. There in her hand was a beautiful corsage, a corsage as delicate and lovely as any you could buy. She leaned over and pinned the pretty flowers on Mrs. Mallory's hospital gown with the safety pin and stood back, cocking her head to study the effect. She adjusted the corsage once more, then reached for the hand mirror on the bed tray. "Perfect," she announced, handing the mirror to her cranky patient. "Wouldn't you agree, Mrs. Mallory?"

The old woman looked at her reflection in the mirror. Slowly, as she studied the pretty flowers bobbing beside her face, a change came over her. She smiled, and a single tear worked its way down her left cheek. "Thank you, dear," she said at last in a tiny voice. "This is the first time in twenty years that I've felt pretty."

Nichole beamed. She looked every bit as happy as Mrs. Mallory. In fact, the elderly patient and the new volunteer were even. After all, it was the first time in her whole life that Nichole Peters had felt useful!

When the group had left Mrs. Mallory's room and were clustered in the hall, everyone began talking at once. "Nichole," Bernie told her, "you sure bailed us all out!"

"Great work, Nick," Shelley exclaimed.

"You were really terrific," Clifford said, his eyes shining with admiration.

Nichole, remembering the way Mrs. Mallory's face had lit up when she saw the corsage, smiled. "Thanks," she told all her friends. "I guess I finally figured out what being a J.V. is all about."

"You certainly did," Mrs. Hurley told her warmly. "And that means this class is officially graduated. You're all ready for work!"

"And for our certificates," Julie reminded her.

"Right," said Mrs. Hurley. "I've asked our Med-Surg Supervisor to meet us in my office for the ceremony." She looked at them proudly. "I invite a different supervisor to meet each class. I like our top nurses to meet our top volunteers!''

Nurse Janet Belmore was not what the J.V.'s expected. A large, heavy woman with a gruff manner, Mercy's Medical-Surgery Supervisor didn't seem the sort of person who chooses nursing as a career. "Is this the group?'' she asked, looking sternly at the teens. "Let's get on with it, Pat. I've got real work waiting.''

Mrs. Hurley handed her six pieces of paper. Barely looking at the certificates, Nurse Belmore read the names off one at a time, handing them quickly to the new volunteers. "There,'' she said when all the certificates had been handed out. "Now it's time to get back to work.'' She walked to the back of the room. "And if you get assigned to my unit, don't expect me to go easy on you just because you're volunteers.'' She turned and headed into the hall without a single handshake or good-bye.

"Don't mind Nurse Belmore,'' Mrs. Hurley cautioned them. "She's a gruff old bear, but she's the best nurse this hospital's ever had.''

"Boy, I sure hope I don't have to work with her,'' Shelley said. "I'd be so nervous, I'd trip all over myself.''

"No need to worry about that yet,'' Mrs. Hurley explained. "Only experienced volunteers work with Janet.'' She put a reassuring arm on Shelley's shoulder. "And they all tell me they never learned so much so fast.''

"Just the same,'' Shelley said, "I think I'd rather start off slow, if it's okay with you.''

The others laughed, and as Mrs. Hurley fastened a gold hospital pin on each volunteer, everyone began to feel more like celebrating. "I think my new volunteers deserve to be treated to ice cream in the snack bar," the Volunteer Director announced. "As your first official duty, you'll be expected to finish a sundae or soda each."

"Now that's the sort of work I'm really good at," Blake said.

"Me, too," agreed Julie. "Just as long as you don't run out of chocolate!"

Seated around a table in Mercy's snack bar, the teens felt relieved and happy. Especially Bernie. She could hardly believe how perfectly everything had worked out. She remembered her fear that Nichole wouldn't fit in at Mercy. Now, looking at her pretty friend, the tiny gold pin with Mercy's lion and lamb sparkling on her collar, Bernie knew Nichole would always bring her own special brand of excitement to patients' lives.

The week of training had flown by, and Bernie wasn't the only one surprised by how far they'd come. "We did it," Clifford said, digging into the butterscotch topping on his sundae. "We actually did it!"

Julie nodded, too excited to touch her soda. "We're actually J.V.'s," she said.

"For a minute there," added Blake, "I was afraid we were all going to flunk out." He grinned broadly at Nichole. "But you saved the day for us with Mrs. Mallory, Nichole."

"You sure came through," agreed Bernie.

"Well, I can't take all the credit," Nichole told them. "Mrs. Hurley helped a lot."

"You mean that little talk you and she had yesterday?" asked Shelley. Like everyone else, she was dying to know what the Volunteer Director had told Nichole. "Did she give you a pep talk or something?"

"In a way." Nichole smiled knowingly, enjoying her secret just a little longer. "But I guess she wouldn't mind my sharing it with you." The others leaned forward eagerly. "Mrs. Hurley told me about the time she threw up on a patient's foot."

"What!" Her friends looked amazed, and even Cliff put down his spoon.

"That's right," Nichole told them. "It seems that when she started work in a hospital, Mrs. Hurley was a nervous basket case just like me." She dipped her spoon into the whipped cream on top of her chocolate sundae, rescuing a cherry from its fluffy depths. "She couldn't stand the sight of blood, and just thinking about germs made her sick."

"Really?" Bernie had trouble picturing the calm, competent Mrs. Hurley upset by anything.

"Yep." Nichole swallowed the cherry, smiling. "On her second day, she had to deliver a gift to a patient with a breathing tube. She took one look at the incision in his throat and got sick all over the poor man's bed!"

Julie and Shelley both looked at their ice cream. Suddenly, they weren't so hungry.

"Mrs. Hurley told me that anyone can get the jitters," Nichole continued, attacking her sundae with relish. "She said some of the best nurses and doctors she's seen started out with the worst cases of nerves."

"It's not where you start out that matters," Clifford told her. "As far as I'm concerned, you ended up at the head of our class!" He looked at Nichole in the same adoring way Teddy always did, and it was pretty clear

65

to everyone at the table that this brainy, quiet J.V. was the newest member of the Nichole Peters fan club!

The O'Connor household was unusually quiet when Bernie got home that afternoon. "The monster's next door at Bobby's," Bernie's mother explained, looking up from a book. "Tracy is visiting a friend from school, and Dad took Sara and Kelly to the car wash."

"For a minute, I thought I'd walked into the wrong house," Bernie laughed. Even though she missed the hustle and bustle of her big family, she was glad to find her mother alone. She couldn't wait to share the excitement of getting her pin and to show her mother the certificate she'd hidden behind her back.

"Look, Mom," she said proudly. "It's official!" She held out the sheet of paper with its fancy, scrolled border and the lacy script she'd read over and over since the presentation.

Mrs. O'Connor marked her place in the book and took the certificate from her daughter. "This is to certify," she read out loud, "that Bernadette O'Connor has completed the prescribed course for Junior Volunteers conducted by Mercy Hospital.

"Congratulations, Honey," she told Bernie. "I know you're going to be a wonderful J.V."

"I'm sure going to try." Bernie took the certificate back and sat beside her mother. She stretched and settled into the couch. "It's been a great day."

"Before I forget," Mrs. O'Connor said, opening her book again, "you got about three phone calls from a very anxious young man." She smiled at Bernie. "It seems he was expecting you at a movie this afternoon."

"Roger?" Bernie felt her buoyant, happy feeling fade

66

away. "But I told him we couldn't make it. He knew we'd be training."

"I guess he didn't get the message." Mrs. O'Connor turned the page of her book. She didn't get many chances to read quietly by herself, and she was determined to make some headway.

"He hasn't been getting the message for weeks." Bernie sighed.

Mrs. O'Connor recognized trouble when she heard it. With a sigh of her own, she closed the book and leaned toward Bernie. "What's wrong?" she asked.

Bernie lay back against one arm of the sofa, slipping her feet out of the chunky white shoes she'd bought for working at Mercy. (Nichole called them "disgusting old lady shoes," but after walking miles of hospital hallways, Bernie was grateful for their thick, cushioned soles.) "I'm not sure anything's wrong," she told her mother. "It's just that something doesn't feel right."

"What do you mean, honey?"

"It's Roger, Mom." Bernie thought of how gentle her gray-eyed chum was, how much fun he was to be with, usually. "He's really sweet and I like him a lot, but he doesn't understand my job at Mercy at all. It's almost as if he wants me to choose between being a J.V. and being his friend."

Mrs. O'Connor frowned. "Roger plays football, doesn't he?" she asked. "Surely, he knows you need to put time into something you really want."

"I guess he just doesn't think volunteering is as important as football," Bernie told her mother. "Every time I talk about Mercy, he makes fun of it." Bernie remembered Roger and Teddy's silly imitations, the way Roger had left their table at Pizza Paradise. "At first, I

67

thought it was harmless teasing, but now it's starting to hurt.''

Mrs. O'Connor put her book on the coffee table and patted her daughter's arm. ''It sounds to me like Roger's pretty fond of you,'' she said. ''Maybe he just needs to know that your work at Mercy won't mean the end of your friendship.''

Bernie wondered if her mother was right. Maybe Roger was just worried, not angry. After all, he *did* walk her to every class, and their friends *were* always joking about his crush on her. ''I've tried to show him that volunteering doesn't mean I'm going to stop living,'' she said. ''I even told Mrs. Hurley I'd rather work on Sundays than Saturdays. That way I can make the JV football games. And I guess I'll be around to help with the laundry, too,'' she added, making a face.

''You couldn't have gotten out of it that easily anyway,'' Mrs. O'Connor teased. ''I would have switched laundry day to Sunday permanently to keep my favorite helper.'' She stood up, tousling her daughter's russet hair. ''Just be patient with Roger,'' she said, heading for the kitchen. ''If he's as nice as you say he is, your doing something that counts will make him like you even more.''

Bernie hoped her mother was right. But when she called Roger back, he sounded curt and stiff. ''You missed a good game,'' he told her. ''But I guess next to General Hospital, it was pretty tame.''

''I'm sorry I missed the game,'' Bernie told him, pulling the long cord from the hall phone into her room and closing the door. ''But I'm not sorry I've finished training. We got our pins and everything.''

''Congratulations.'' Roger's voice was flat, as if he

really didn't mean it. "I guess that means you're a full-time nurse and an ex-football fan, huh?"

Bernie remembered what her mother had said about patience. "It means I'm a J.V. who won't be working on Saturdays, Rog." She put the phone on her bed and sprawled across the pretty, apple-green spread. "It means I'll be working one or two days after school, and that I won't have to miss a single football game."

"Really?" He sounded a little friendlier now, a little more like the Roger Bernie was used to.

"Really," she assured him. "In fact, I'm looking forward to both Hayward games next Saturday."

"Both?"

"Sure," she said. "Remember, I told you I work with Blake Willard, Hayward's varsity captain?"

"Oh, yeah," Roger said, his voice falling back into the mocking tone she'd heard at Pizza Paradise. "Doctor Jock."

"I promised him I'd be in the stands, even if I'd have to root against his team."

"Musn't let the Doctor down."

"Wouldn't it be neat if we could all get together after the games?" Bernie asked.

"Hey, count me out," Roger told her. "I wouldn't think of interfering with your date."

"Roger, it's not a date," Bernie insisted. "We're just friends."

"Right," Roger said. "Just like you and me."

"No, not like that." Bernie rolled over on her back, staring at the silver stars she'd pasted on her ceiling, wishing it were dark enough for them to glow. "I don't know Blake nearly as well as I know you."

"With all the time you two will be spending together," Roger said, "it won't be long before you know him a lot better."

"Roger, what's up?" asked Bernie. "I thought you'd be glad about the schedule I worked out. I thought you'd understand how exciting Mercy is."

"I understand, all right," Roger said. "I understand you don't need boring old friends like me anymore."

"Rog, you know that's crazy," Bernie told him. "Ridge Dale just wouldn't mean anything without you and the gang."

Roger's voice had turned sulky, like a hurt child's. "Well, we're all glad you can fit us into your busy schedule."

"Roger!" Bernie was losing the good feeling she'd had at the pinning. All she felt now was confused. "That's not fair. I . . ."

"I've got to go." Roger cut her off. "My family's waiting for me. It's party time."

"Oh, that's right," Bernie remembered. "Say Happy Birthday to your dad."

"Sure." There was a pause. "And you say hi to your friend, Doctor Do-Good."

"Roger, wait . . ." Bernie heard a harsh click as Roger hung up the phone, then she felt her eyes begin to fill. Why did everything have to be so mixed up lately? She reached for the certificate she'd put on her desk, then stared at the delicate, scrolled lettering. *This is to certify,* she thought, *that Bernadette O'Connor has learned a lot about nursing, but she still can't figure out boys!* What was wrong with Roger, anyway? Would she find him sitting, smiling and warm as ever, across from the lunch table on Monday? Or would she face a stranger—an angry, unreasonable boy she hardly knew at all?

7

Battle-ax Belmore

"I don't care what anyone thinks," Nichole insisted, weaving her way through the Monday lunch crowd in the Ridge Dale cafeteria. "If I feel like wearing my J.V. uniform to school, I will!" Her hair pulled back in a tight bun, the new volunteer looked striking in her simple striped tunic.

"But aren't you afraid of getting teased?" asked Shelley. "Even Mariah doesn't wear her uniform to school."

"I'm not a fashion *follower*," Nichole said, putting her tray down at their usual table. "I'm a fashion *leader*. Besides," she added, smoothing the back of her skirt before she sat down, "I refuse to keep this darling uniform folded up in my locker all day. I'd rather be teased than wrinkled!"

Bernie couldn't help smiling. Only a few days ago,

Nichole had been complaining about the outfit she now wore so proudly. "You know what?" she asked. "Nichole's right. This could start a whole new trend!"

"Well, I know something that won't." Shelley frowned and put her hero sandwich down. "What's in these Ridge Dale combos, anyway?"

"I'm sure this is cheese and I guess this is ham," said Bernie, prying open her own hero and combing through its contents. "But I'll be darned if I have a clue what this is!" She pulled a limp strand out of the roll, draping it across her plate. "I think Teddy's right," she added, smiling. "Combos are how the cafeteria gets rid of leftovers."

"Speaking of Teddy," Shelley said, looking across the table at the two empty seats the friends had saved, "where do you suppose he and Sourpuss are?"

Bernie looked suddenly thoughtful. "If you mean Roger," she said, "I don't think he's too eager to run into me. We had sort of a fight over the phone this weekend."

"Let me guess." Shelley noticed her friend's worried expression, remembered how badly Roger had acted at Pizza Paradise. "He's still bent out of shape about Mercy, right?"

Bernie sighed, her green eyes scanning the cafeteria, looking for a familiar tall figure with a shock of ash blond hair. "I'm afraid so," she told Shelley. She didn't mention Blake or the way Roger had hung up so quickly. "He doesn't want to hear about the hospital at all."

"Well, I do," Bev Feldon announced, standing with a loaded tray behind them. "Mind if I join you?" The trim majorette headed toward one of the two empty seats just as Bernie noticed Roger and Teddy leaving the cafeteria line. She saw them glance in her direction, then turn to join another table across the room. Had they seen Bev? Or was Roger deliberately avoiding her?

"Neat uniform!" Bev said, as Nichole beamed. "Now tell me everything," Bev invited, sitting down and unloading her tray. "I want to hear all about what you'll be doing at Mercy on your first day." Suddenly, though, she stopped talking and stared at her three friends. "Oh, no!" she gasped. "I'm so stupid. Look at me gabbing away with my brain on autopilot."

Usually poised, Bev was so flustered she could hardly speak. "I . . . I just didn't think," she stammered. She studied Nichole, then she glanced at Bernie and Shelley. "I just assumed you all passed the training." She touched Bernie's arm. "Oh, Bern, I'm so sorry," she blurted.

Bernie was puzzled. "Sorry for what?" she asked. "What on earth do you mean, Bev?"

Bev's voice dropped to an embarrassed whisper, and her cheeks colored. "I mean I never dreamed you and Shelley would flunk out of the training," she said. "I'm sorry Nichole's the only one that passed." Now she turned again to Nichole. "No, no. That's not what I mean either," she explained, flushing deeper. "I'm not sorry you made it, Nichole. I'm just sorry the others didn't."

"But they did, silly," Nichole told her, finally realizing what had caused the confusion. She touched the starched skirt of her J.V. tunic. "I'm the only one in uniform because Mrs. Hurley asked me to come in today and work on flower arrangements." She paused, remembering how happy Mrs. Mallory had been with her corsage. "She says I have a magic touch," she added.

"That's right," Shelley explained. "We all work together Thursdays and Sundays." She lifted the roll off the top of her combo once more, sniffed, then pushed her plate away. "But it seems Mercy can't do without their famous floral designer on Mondays."

Nichole, obviously proud, blushed. It was good to feel needed.

"You have all the luck," Bernie smiled fondly at her friend. "You won't be in Orthopedics with Shelley and me tomorrow."

"What do you mean?" asked Nichole. "Isn't that where all the handsome jocks with sprained ankles and bad knees get sent?"

"It's also where Battle-ax Belmore is stationed," Shelley told her. "Remember her? She gave us our certificates."

Nichole recalled the heavy nurse with the steel-gray hair and the stern face. "Gosh," she said, "I thought she only worked with experienced J.V.'s."

"It seems the Ortho head nurse is on vacation," Shelley explained. "And Belmore's taking her place."

"Well, I'm just glad you all made the J.V. squad, after all," Bev told them, smiling with relief. "For a minute there, I thought I'd made a major PR goof."

"Speaking of major goofs," interrupted Nichole, nodding toward the back of the cafeteria. "Look who decided they were too good to sit with us."

Now everyone turned to see what Bernie had noticed earlier. There at a distant table sat Teddy and Roger. Even though Bernie was sure that four pairs of eyes burning into them would force one of the boys to turn

74

around, neither Roger nor Teddy looked in their direction. "It's pretty packed in here today," she said quickly. "Maybe they didn't see us."

"Bern," said Shelley firmly. "We're sitting at the same table we always sit at, and we saved the same two seats we always do." She stared more intently at the boys, frowning. "Face it, Roger's talked Teddy into a boycott."

"How childish can you get?" Bev shook her head. "But why would Teddy go along with Roger? I didn't think Teddy let anyone do his thinking for him."

Just as if he'd heard her words, Teddy turned around and looked straight at the girls' table. He shrugged his shoulders, then pointed to Roger, who still kept his back to them. Now Teddy made circles in the air next to his head to signal how crazy he thought his friend was acting.

"I guess Teddy's trying to apologize for Roger," Shelley decided, waving across the room to him.

"Apology *not* accepted," Nichole said firmly. "Long distance doesn't count." She scooped up her tray as the bell rang. "Come on," she urged. "Who cares about those two anyway?"

The others stood, gathering up their trays, getting ready for sixth period. *I do,* thought Bernie. *I care.* Her heart sank as she watched Roger head for the exit without looking back. Then, unusually quiet, she joined her friends in the long line that was filing out the door.

That night, when Nichole phoned her after work, Bernie could practically see her friend's broad, satisfied grin. "Being a J.V. is absolutely and totally too wonderful," she reported breathlessly. "I made four special flower arrangements this afternoon. And I got four rave reviews."

"That's great," said Bernie warmly. She wished she felt half as bright and happy as Nichole sounded.

"And it was such fun to deliver them with Cliff and Julie!" Nichole was so excited, she never even heard the depressed edge in Bernie's voice. "I'm so glad we arranged our schedules so I work with them on Mondays. It made going in without you and Shelley a lot easier."

"Terrific," responded Bernie. She knew how much it meant to Nichole to have friends around her.

"I already feel at home," bubbled Nichole. "I gave two different visitors directions. Oh, Bernie, I wish I could work at Mercy every day!"

"I'll bet you do," laughed Bernie. "Then you'd never have to do homework."

"I'm serious, Bern," Nichole insisted. "I'm thinking about becoming a nurse."

Bernie knew how impetuous Nichole could be, how she was always rushing headlong into projects and then abandoning them or leaving them for others to finish. But somehow, this time was different. There was a new determination in her friend's tone. "Maybe you will, Nichole," she said. "Maybe you will."

But when the two had hung up, and Bernie had gone back to the same geometry problem she'd already spent twenty minutes on, things seemed a lot less cheerful than they had a moment before. Two faces kept getting in the way, floating between Bernie and her geometry book. First Nurse Belmore, deep, angry frown marks running down each side of her mouth, stared fiercely at Bernie. "Don't expect me to go easy on you," she

76

growled, just as she had when she'd given the volunteers their certificates.

Bernie groaned, forcing herself to focus on the isosceles triangle behind Nurse Belmore. "I'll never finish this assignment," she sighed to herself, blinking, hoping the page would stop dancing and the diagram would finally begin to make sense. "Heck, I'll never even finish this problem!" Then, as the triangle finally started to get clearer and Nurse Belmore's face faded away, another took its place—just as angry, glaring at her in the same harsh way. "I'm glad *someone* can depend on you," Roger told her. "I just wish your friends could!"

Dressing the next morning didn't take any thought at all. Bernie got to wear her J.V. uniform to school! After all, Shelley and she had decided, if Nichole could be brave enough to wear her tunic to school, why couldn't they? "You look fantastic," Shelley greeted her friend as the two spotted each other outside Ridge Dale's huge oak front door.

Bernie pushed through the crowd of students laughing and gossiping in the chilly fall air. "You don't look too shabby yourself," she said when she reached Shelley's side. She could just see the stripes of Shelley's uniform peeking out from under her navy coat. "We're going to do the best job ever in Ortho."

"If Belmore lets us," Shelley told her. She waved to some girls across the broad brick courtyard where everyone waited for the first bell, then leaned closer to her friend. "To tell you the truth, Bernie," she confided, "I've been really uptight about working with Nurse Belmore. I'm so afraid I'll drop something, a bandage or a water carafe—or a patient!"

"You're not the only one," Bernie admitted, remembering how worries about Nurse Belmore and Roger had made her geometry homework take twice as long as usual. "But there are two of us and only one of her." She put her arm around her friend. "We're in this together, right?"

"Am I ever glad," Shelley told her. "If I had to face that old grump alone, I don't know what I'd do!"

Bernie knew just how Shelley felt. In fact, she was very grateful she had friends to help her through the long day ahead. In geometry, she sat next to Mariah Tecknor, the senior who had helped them get their jobs at Mercy. It was good to be able to confide her worries about working with Nurse Belmore to Mariah, good to hear the pretty dark-haired girl laugh and tell her Belmore's bark was a lot worse than her bite. "Don't listen to her," Mariah advised. "Just watch her. She's not a patient teacher, but she's the best nurse ever."

It was good, too, to have Shelley and Nichole and Bev Feldon and plump, funny Elise Sheridan to help her get through lunch—without Roger. Again, her ex-friend ignored her, walking right past their group to join Brian and his crowd at another table. "Well, that clinches it," remarked Nichole, watching Roger and Teddy walk past them. "I vote we expel those two from our lunch club."

"Lunch club?" asked Bev. "I didn't know you had a lunch club."

"We don't," Nichole told her. "But I vote we start one so we can kick them out."

"I vote we kick them out and take their desserts," Elise recommended. "This blueberry cheesecake is awesome!"

As she laughed with the others, Bernie forgot for a little while how hurt she felt. And by the time eighth period ended and it was time to meet Shelley in the courtyard again, there was nothing on her mind but Mercy. Nurse Belmore or not, she was looking forward to her first J.V. assignment.

After the girls had signed in at the hospital's Volunteer Office, they headed for the Orthopedics Unit. Janet Belmore was waiting for them. She was seated at the unit nursing station, her eyes glued to the thick, black watch on her wrist. "Do you know what time it is?" she asked them, without looking up.

Shelley and Bernie looked at each other, then shrugged. They had been careful to arrive at Mercy promptly at three-thirty. What had they done wrong?

"Well?" Nurse Belmore glared at the two now.

"We volunteered to work from three-thirty to six," Bernie told her finally. "We thought we were right on time."

"You're not." Nurse Belmore stood up and walked from behind the station. "It's three-thirty-five." She turned and started marching down the hall without even looking back. Shelley and Bernie exchanged glances again and hurried after her. "From now on, make sure you sign in and arrive at your assigned unit on time."

They followed her to a supply closet, where another volunteer was waiting for them. She had a round, child's face and wore her hair in a high ponytail. "Hi," she greeted them nervously.

"This is Miss McClure," Nurse Belmore said stiffly. "Miss McClure, meet Miss O'Connor and Miss Jansen." She turned to the closet and handed down sets of linen. "The three of you will be working together this afternoon."

When the girls each had an armful of sheets and towels and pillowcases, Nurse Belmore led them back down the hall. "Your first assignment is to change the beds in rooms 304 through 312. I expect you to finish by four o'clock when patients will be returning from physical therapy."

As their gruff supervisor strode off down the hall, Bernie whispered, "If you call us Miss O'Connor and Miss Jansen, we won't answer you, Miss McClure." She smiled at the shocked look on the anxious girl's face. "I'm Bernie and this is Shelley."

The girl grinned, more at ease now. "Hi," she told them with relief. "My name's Tara." She dropped a pillowcase from the top of her pile, and the three of them went back to the closet for a fresh one. "Sorry," she explained. "I've never worked with anyone as tough as Nurse Belmore. I'm pretty nervous."

"*You're* nervous!" laughed Shelley. "We're paralyzed! This is our very first day as volunteers."

"Oh, gosh," the girl exclaimed. "I've been here nearly a year, and she still gives me goose bumps."

"Well," said Shelley, winking at Bernie. "Just remember, there are three of us and only one of her. We're in this together!"

And she was right. As the three girls moved quickly from empty room to room, stripping the old sheets off each bed, setting out new clean towels, they began to feel like friends. By the time they'd finished room 312, it was only ten minutes to four, and they were feeling quite relaxed and confident. Shelley brushed a hand across the taut, crisply folded blanket on the window

80

bed. "Looks just like the ones in training, doesn't it?" she asked proudly.

"It sure does," Tara agreed, her glossy ponytail bouncing. "We make quite a team."

Behind them, a stern voice interrupted. "Quite a team of chatterers," Nurse Belmore observed dryly. "If you finish a task early, don't stand around congratulating yourselves." She walked into the room, and ran her own hand over the blanket. "There's always more work to be done."

The rest of the afternoon was all work and no play. The three girls filled water carafes, ran back and forth to Central Supply, distributed dinner trays, and helped feed patients who couldn't manage by themselves. By the time they signed out at the Volunteer Office, each of them felt as if she'd run a marathon. "Well," sighed Tara as they walked together to the hospital entrance, "I'm glad the Ortho nurse gets back tomorrow. Nurse Belmore is really rough!"

"She sure is," agreed Bernie. "But I really like the way she puts the patients first."

"Yep," agreed Shelley. "She may be all business with us, but did you see how gentle she was with that girl in 210, the one with the broken leg?"

"And with Mr. Saunders in 212," added Tara. "She took all that time just to explain how his hip surgery was going to work. You could see he felt a lot better afterwards."

The three of them talked a while longer, eager to share their excitement and relief. Tara invited her new friends for a soda in the snack bar, but Shelley had mountains of homework and Bernie had to get home to babysit monster Mathew while her parents went for a

81

rare dinner out. "We'll take a rain check," Bernie promised Tara. "Since we all three work Tuesdays, we're bound to be on the same unit again soon."

On the way home, Shelley sounded as if she could hardly wait for their next day at Mercy. "Wow," she told Bernie, "we just lived through Battle-ax! We can handle anything now!"

"Did you hear what Miss Henley in 306 said about her soft sheets?" asked Bernie, grinning.

"How about Mrs. Hopkins in 311?" bubbled Shelley. "She said she never could have eaten left-handed without my help!"

Bernie beamed. She remembered how nervous she'd been about today's assignment. She could hardly believe how good she felt now. "We made a difference, Shelley!" she said, whirling in happy circles as she walked. "We really made a difference!"

At home, Bernie remembered Shelley's description of feeding the patient with a broken arm as she forced the last spoonful of broccoli down her squirmy brother's throat. "Hey, you!" she protested. "You promised Mom you'd clean your plate before you watched *Squirrels in Orbit.*" But Mathew wasn't listening, he was already streaking out of the kitchen to watch his favorite TV show.

Bernie sighed. She turned to the sink, grateful when her sister Tracy offered to help with the dishes. "I want to hear more about Nurse Belmore," the ten year old begged, pouring too much dishwashing liquid into the water Bernie had run. "Me, too! Me, too!" chimed in little Kelly and Sara, struggling from the table, each carrying her plate.

The dishes were nearly finished and Bernie had just started her story for the second time, telling her sisters again about Nurse Belmore's lecture on tardiness, when the phone rang. It was Shelley and something was definitely wrong.

"Bernie," Shelley groaned into the receiver. "The worst thing in the world just happened."

"What's the matter?" Bernie asked, handing the last plate to Tracy and motioning the others out of the kitchen.

"Oh, Bernie. I can't be a J.V. anymore!" Shelley sounded awful, her voice tight and high.

"Not be a volunteer?" Bernie watched Tracy rinse the plate and put it in the dryer. "What on earth do you mean, Shelley Jansen?"

"It's my dad," her friend explained. "He just phoned from work. He said one of his friends has offered me a job at his store. I'd have to work after school and weekends." Shelley choked on her words, as if she were out of breath. "Oh, Bernie," she asked, "what am I going to do?"

Tracy left the kitchen to join her brother and sisters in the TV room, and Bernie sank into a chair by the window. "I don't know, Shelley," she said. She remembered the excitement in Shelley's eyes when she'd announced that if they'd survived Nurse Belmore, they could get through anything. "I just don't know."

"He wants me to start next week," moaned Shelley. "He sounded so happy, I wanted to cry!"

"Next week?" Bernie couldn't imagine working at Mercy without Shelley. Suddenly, she felt angry and hurt, as if she were losing still another friend. "When would we ever see each other?" she asked.

"Hardly ever," gasped Shelley. "Oh, Bernie!"

"You've got to tell him how you feel," Bernie decided. "Maybe if he knows how much Mercy means to us, if he understands what we do . . ."

"No good," said Shelley firmly. "We need the extra money badly. I have to help out if I can." She paused, and Bernie thought she heard her friend sob softly into the phone. "I just have to, that's all."

"But, that's not fair," Bernie protested. "You love working at Mercy. And I love working with you." She tried to think of a solution, anything that might help. "We'll find a way, Shelley."

"There is no way," Shelley said quietly. "I can't go back to Mercy after this week." She sighed. "There's nothing anyone can do."

8

Shelley Speaks Up

"My life is ruined," Shelley announced at lunch the next day. "I've only got one more day at Mercy!" Her tray, full of food, sat untouched in front of her. Bernie had never seen her friend look so discouraged.

Nichole noticed the change in Shelley, too. And she decided to take charge. "No prob," she told the pretty brunette. "I know how to handle dads. Leave everything to me."

"Thanks, Nick," Shelley said. "But I'm afraid my father isn't going to give in on this one." She knew that spoiled Nichole was used to getting anything she wanted from her wealthy parents. "We really need the extra money."

"All you have to do," advised Nichole, "is look tragic." She brushed her blond hair off her face, slumping forward in her seat. She pouted unhappily, her full lips turning down, her eyes, the exact same blue as her thick angora sweater, filling with tears. "Like this," she said.

Bernie studied her friend's orphan pose, then burst out laughing. "Why, Nichole Peters," she exclaimed, "if I didn't know better, I'd swear you were about to cry!"

"I am, Daddy," Nichole said, her voice thin and small. "If you make me leave those poor little children in Pediatrics and those helpless senior citizens in Long Term Care, I know I'll just die." She clasped her slender hands together, closing her long lashes over her eyes. "They need me so, Daddy." Her eyes opened again, huger than ever. "And I need them."

"Hey, Fair Damsel," a voice behind her asked, "what's the problem?" Teddy Hollins, looking concerned, was standing near their table. "Anything this handsome knight can do?"

Nichole, her performance interrupted, suddenly brightened and dug into her burger. "No, thanks," she said breezily without looking up at Teddy. "I don't need any favors from people who hang out with people who are acting like spoiled babies."

"You mean Roger?" Teddy asked. He looked at Bernie, apology written all over his face. "Gee, I know he's acting like a jerk. I've tried to talk some sense into him, but he's not listening to anyone lately."

Bernie smiled at Teddy, moving a tray aside for him. "Hey, it's not your fault," she said, glad to have at least one friend back again. "Sit down and cheer this gloomy table up."

Teddy hesitated, then turned to look at a table toward the back of the crowded cafeteria. Following his glance,

Bernie saw Roger, his back to them, eating with some frosh football players. "Gee," Teddy said, "I'd like to. I've missed you guys."

"So?" Shelley challenged him. "Why not sit down?"

"Why not is right!" Teddy grinned and slipped into the seat beside Nichole. "I may be losing one friend this way, but I'm gaining three." He glanced again across the cafeteria. "Roger wanted me to boycott your do-good phase. Heck, I'd rather boycott his pig-headed phase."

"Roger asked you not to see us?" Shelley stood up from the table, her hands on her hips. Bernie and Nichole turned to stare at him. "He actually said that?"

"Sort of," Teddy told her. "He's sure you're just playing nurse, and if we give you time, you'll realize who your real friends are."

"We do!" Shelley threw her napkin down and strode away from the table.

"Shelley," Bernie called after her friend, "where are you going?"

"I'm going to give someone a piece of my mind," Shelley said over her shoulder. "Someone who doesn't know the meaning of the word friend!" She walked briskly away, headed straight for the table where Roger was eating with his teammates.

Nichole, Teddy, and Bernie watched, open-mouthed, as Shelley approached Roger, then stood beside him, arms folded, foot tapping like a teacher waiting for an answer. They watched as a crowd gathered around the team table, Shelley and Roger speaking angrily to each other. The table was too far away to hear what they

87

were saying, but it was soon clear that Roger had heard enough.

Suddenly, he stood up from the table, his tray in his hands. He turned his back on Shelley and walked briskly away. When one of the players at his table called him, holding up the books he'd left behind, Roger turned around. But he didn't stop walking! Still angry, forgetting to watch where he was going, the accident-prone athlete plowed right into another table! Trays and food and Roger went flying.

Shelley didn't stay to help clean up. As some students scraped tuna salad out of their laps and others thronged around Roger, helping him to his feet and rescuing his tray from halfway across the room, Shelley marched back to where her friends sat in stunned silence.

"I guess I told that lamebrain," she announced, sitting down and digging into her meal with relish.

"Boy!" said Teddy. "When you tell somebody something, I guess he gets the message!"

"Is Roger okay?" Bernie saw the crowd gathering around Roger, watched him stand and brush off his chinos. "Did he hurt himself?"

"Will you stop worrying about him?" begged Nichole. "Roger the Klutz can take care of himself. He's used to walking into things."

"Face it, Bern," Shelley said between mouthfuls. "Off the field, that boy is an accident waiting to happen." She smiled apologetically. "Besides, all I did was tell him the truth."

"What on earth did you say to him, Shell?"

"The same thing I'm going to tell my father tonight when he gets home," Shelley said calmly.

Bernie and Teddy and Nichole looked at each other,

then at Roger, who was glaring, red-faced and indignant, at the back of Shelley's head. But Shelley never turned around. She continued eating, suddenly enjoying her food. "Pass the salt, would you, Bern," she asked without looking up.

"Sure, Shell." Bernie pushed the salt cellar across the table and waited. "Well?" she asked impatiently.

"Well, what?"

"What are you going to tell your dad?"

Shelley looked at her friends and said in a new, firm voice, "I'm going to tell him that there are plenty of kids—and grownups, too, for that matter—who sit around and complain about things." She took a sip of soda, then added, "I'm going to tell him that Bernie and Nichole and I have a chance to do more than just talk. We can actually make things better. And I'm going to tell him that when a chance like that comes along, people who care about you shouldn't stand in your way."

"But, Shell," interrupted Nichole. "I thought you already told your dad how much Mercy means to you."

"I didn't have the nerve," Shelley confessed. "I mean, Dad works so hard, and he worries so much about being able to provide for Mom and me." She sighed, then folded her arms. "But you know what? Our work at Mercy is too special to give up. It's more important than anything—even money."

Her three friends stared at her. They saw the color in her cheeks, the light in her coffee-colored eyes. "Wow!" said Teddy, standing up as the sixth period bell sounded. "Where do I sign up?" Everyone laughed, except Shelley. "I hope my dad feels the same way," she said quietly. "I hope he understands."

*   *   *

The next day, when the three Ridge Dale volunteers reported for duty at Mercy's Volunteer Office, they learned they would be spending the afternoon on the Pediatric Unit. Because children's parents and families visited frequently, volunteers weren't assigned to Peeds as often as they were to other units. So the girls should have been happy at this rare chance to work with young patients. They should also have been thrilled to find that the other J.V. working in the unit with them was their friend Julie, from training class. But no one could get very excited about anything. Not with Shelley so depressed.

Gloom settled like a cloud around their normally cheerful friend. "This is my last day here," she kept moaning. "I can't believe I'll have to turn in my uniform this afternoon."

Nichole was confused. "I thought you were going to set your dad straight," she said. "Didn't you tell him how important being a hospital volunteer is?"

"Yes."

"So, what's the problem?" Nichole persisted.

"The problem is he cried." Shelley looked defeated, as unhappy as they'd ever seen her. She remembered her father's worried face, the way his eyes had filled with tears when she told him how much she loved working at Mercy.

Bernie touched her shoulder. "You don't have to tell us if you don't feel like it, Shell," she said gently.

Julie stood off to one side, feeling helpless. "Would you rather I left you guys alone?" she asked.

Shelley smiled gamely, squeezing the tall girl's hand.

"No, silly," she said. "You stay right here. I need all the support I can get."

Julie seemed relieved. She put her finger to her lips, then led her three friends briskly down the hall and into an empty room. "The floor nurse asked me to make up this bed for a new patient. If we all work together the job will go faster." She smiled slyly at Shelley. "And while we're working, you can tell us everything and we'll come up with a way to help."

Shelley sank gratefully into a chair by the window bed, while the others unfolded the pile of sheets and towels that were waiting on the bed. "I know we're not supposed to talk on duty," she told them. "But I really do want to get this off my chest."

"Go for it," Nichole urged, while Bernie and Julie shook out the bottom sheet and smoothed it over the mattress pad.

"It's just that my dad really, really needs me to help out with expenses," Shelley confided. "He still sends my mom money every month, and he's having a lot of trouble making ends meet.

"The bad part is," she added, "that he's not being mean. He says he understands what being a J.V. means to me. He hugged me when I told him about feeding Mrs. Hopkins in Ortho." Shelley stopped, choking back a sob of her own. "He said he wished we could find a way to cut expenses so I could work at Mercy, but. . . ." Her voice trailed away. She studied her hands in her lap.

"Looks like you've got a welcoming committee," announced a cheerful voice outside room 28. Ruth Wiley, the Peeds Floor Nurse, poked her head in the door, then pushed a wheelchair into the room. "Jason,"

91

she said to the curly-headed youngster in the chair, "I don't know how these four knew you were going to be coming up from recovery, but I'll bet some friendly faces are just what you need."

"Hi," said Shelley, scrambling out of the chair and holding out her hand to the little boy in the wheelchair. "I'm Shelley, and these are my friends, Nichole, Bernie, and Julie."

Jason's face lit up and he leaned forward to shake hands. "Hi," he said in a growly voice, then frowned and raised his hand to his throat.

"I wouldn't try to talk right now," advised Nurse Wiley. "That tonsilectomy means you won't be able to do much with your throat for a while." She paused, smiling. "Except eat ice cream."

Bernie couldn't help thinking how glad she was that it was Nurse Wiley, and *not* Janet Belmore, who'd found the four of them chatting in Jason's room! Gratefully, she walked to the pretty young nurse's side. "Shall I go down to Dietary and see if I can get a scoop of dutch chocolate?" she asked, anxious to help.

"Sounds like a good idea to me," Nurse Wiley told her. "How about you, Jason?"

Jason's blue eyes lit up under his pale, wispy curls. His smile told Bernie all she needed to know. She turned on her heels and headed down to Dietary, leaving Jason with his lively welcoming committee.

When she returned with a thick mound of ice cream in a silver dish, she found Jason tucked comfortably in bed, with Shelley reading to him.

"Where'd everyone go?" Bernie asked.

Shelley looked up from the book, a fairy tale book with the picture of a giant on its cover. "They're mak-

92

ing the rest of the beds on the floor," she told Bernie. But Miss Wiley said I could finish this story first." She turned back to the page. "And then the prince took his sword from its sheath," she read. " 'I challenge you to fight, Evil Troll,' he roared."

"How about some ice cream with your story, Jason?" Bernie asked, stepping up to the bed and putting the dish on Jason's tray. The little boy turned and smiled. "Thanks," he whispered in his froggy voice, then turned back to Shelley and the book. "Then what happened, Shelley?" he asked, his cheeks flushed with excitement.

Shelley winked at Bernie who tiptoed out of the room. "The troll bellowed a horrible bellow," Shelley read while Jason stared fascinated at the illustration. "You are not worthy to fight the likes of me!"

When Bernie found Julie and Nichole they had made up the last bed. "Nice timing," said Nichole, teasing. "We've finished without you."

"Looks like I'm not the only one who's getting out of bed-making," smiled Bernie. "Shelley and Jason make quite a tcam, don't they?"

"Yep," agreed Julie. "Nurse Wiley said Shelley's doing more good in there than if she made every bed in the hospital." Julie grinned good-naturedly, smoothing the blanket on the last bed.

"Jason seems to be helping her, too," Nichole observed. "I'd say she's forgotten all about her problems with her dad."

When the three saw Nurse Wiley striding towards them from down the hall, they decided it was time to stop gossiping. "What's next?" Bernie asked, cheerfully.

"Menus," said Nurse Wiley, handing them a clipboard with the diet list and a handful of menu blanks. "Now don't forget to check to see if patients are on regular or special diets, then let them make their choices for dinner. If they can't fill out the menus, you can do it for them." She handed the papers to the girls. "When you're finished, turn all the forms into me at reception. Any questions?"

"Is Shelley excused again?" asked Nichole. You could tell she was getting tired of doing all the work, while Shelley played with Jason.

Nurse Wiley laughed. "I guess so," she said. "Jason's parents are out of town, and I think he's taken a real liking to his substitute mom. I can't pry the two of them apart!"

"It seems to me," Nichole whispered to Julie and Bernie as the three girls started down the hall with the menus, "that dinner is one duty our Home Ec star shouldn't wriggle out of." She stopped outside room 28, and none of them could help giggling as they listened to Shelly's fierce troll voice. "Stand back, pathetic princeling," she read from the book to Jason. "Or I will have royal meat for my stew tonight."

"And Shelley will probably help him with the recipe!" Nichole strode off to the next room with her menu blanks, leaving her two friends behind.

"Is Shelley really that good a cook?" asked Julie, peeking in the room, watching Jason, eyes gleaming, listening to the story.

"Ask Clarisse," Bernie told her, smiling.

"Clarisse?" Julie looked puzzled.

"Clarisse is Shelley's cat," Bernie explained. "She's

94

Shell's chief taster, and she's the world's fattest, happiest feline!''

When all the menus had been collected, it was time to go home. There was only one problem—Jason. As her three friends waited at the door to Jason's room, the little boy begged Shelley to stay. "You can't go," he told her. "You're my favorite nurse. And you have to read me what happens next."

Shelley laughed, but she couldn't help feeling proud of the way Jason's eyes shone when he looked at her. And the way he'd called her *nurse*! "We've already read this story four times," she told him. "I don't think it's going to turn out any differently this time. How about if I ask Nurse Wiley to finish up for me?"

"No," Jason insisted. He held onto Shelley's hand. "I want *you* to read it to me."

Bernie noticed that he hadn't even finished his ice cream. "Hey, Jason," she said. "Shelley's family needs her, too." Then, calmly, she added, "But she'll be back this weekend."

Suddenly, it seemed, all Shelley's problems raced back into her mind. She looked miserable again. Her sad expression said everything. She wouldn't be back this weekend. Or ever again.

But Jason was delighted. He relaxed his tight grip on Shelley's arm. "Promise?" he said. "Promise you'll be back?"

"Yes!" Nichole told him, walking into the room and dragging Shelley away. "She does promise." Despite Shelley's warning look, Nichole took cheerful charge of everything. She scooped up a spoonful of ice cream and put it in Jason's mouth. "If you eat your ice cream,"

she said gaily. "Don't worry now, Jason. Get plenty of rest and Shelley will be back before you know it!"

"Okay," agreed Jason, beaming. "Bye, Shelley," he tried to yell, then grabbed his throat. "Bye," he whispered this time. "See you soon."

"How could you *do* that?" asked Shelley when all four girls had checked off the floor and were headed down to the Volunteer Office to sign out. "How could you lie to a little kid?" Her voice was angry, sharp. "You know I won't be back. I have to start my job this weekend."

But Nichole, all confidence, just ignored her friend's confusion. "I'm willing to bet, Shelley Jansen," she said breezily, "that this is *not* your last day at Mercy."

The others stopped behind her. Julie smiled, and Bernie slipped her arm through Shelley's. "What is it?" Shelley asked, puzzled. "What are you three up to?"

"Just a little surefire solution Julie came up with when we were passing out menus," Bernie told her.

Shelley turned hopefully to their new friend. "Solution? What is it, Julie?"

Julie grinned shyly. "Filling out those dinner menus gave me a delicious idea," she said.

"Don't forget, Julie," Nichole interrupted. "It was Bernie and me who told you what a great cook Shelley is."

"Right," Julie admitted. "And if you're half as good as they say you are, Shelley, you just may be able to cook up the answer to all your problems!"

9

"Give Me an R!"

Shelley was still upset with her friends for lying to Jason. She couldn't understand why Nichole, Julie, and Bernie were all smiles, why they insisted on stopping off at the hospital snack bar before they went home.

"I don't know what there is to celebrate," Shelley told them, as they took seats around a booth at the side of the snack bar. "Unless you think tricking a little boy is something to be proud of."

But the other girls were full of good spirits, especially Julie. Everyone ordered sodas and Julie ordered a slice of apple pie. When it came, she turned to Shelley. "How many smiling faces do you see in this room?" She paused, glancing around the nearly empty snack bar. "For that matter, how many faces do you see?"

"Not many," Shelley admitted, taking the root beer float the waitress handed her.

"Want to know why?" Julie asked, putting the plate of apple pie in front of Shelley. "Just try this." Shelley looked confused. "Go on," Julie urged. "Take a bite."

Shelley shrugged, dug her fork into the pie, and swallowed a bite. It was stale and tasteless. "I guess the food here is one thing about Mercy that's less than perfect," she said.

"Exactly!" Julie sounded as if bad food were good news. "Why, I even heard a lady say she always filled up before she came to Mercy, just so she wouldn't have to eat at the snack bar!"

Shelley laughed and pushed the plate of pie away. "I can't blame her," she said.

"But you should thank her," replied Julie, grinning. "Because it's people like her who are going to help you keep your job at Mercy!"

Shelley put her soda glass down and looked at Julie. "What do you mean?" she asked.

"I mean," Julie explained, "a snack bar is no good without snacks."

"Snacks?"

"That's why we're going to spend this weekend helping you cook up some of those fabulous desserts you've been creating for Home Ec."

"You mean all the cakes and cookies that have given Clarisse her spare tire?" Shelley was still confused.

"From now on," Bernie told her, smiling, "you'll be cooking for someone else besides that overweight tabby of yours."

"Who do you mean?"

"Why, visitors to Mercy, of course." Bernie's smile was broader than ever. "But first, you'll have to treat some VIPs to a taste test."

"What VIPs?" Shelley looked from one girl to the other. "Will someone *please* tell me what's going on?"

Now Nichole leaned forward across the marble-topped table. "I'll help you decorate the cakes and cookies." Her face was eager, excited. "I see blue ribbons of sugar with little candy flowers."

Bernie, too, was caught up in their plans. "And I'll bring you my mom's recipe for butterscotch brownies. If that doesn't persuade them, nothing will!"

"Persuade who?" Shelley asked.

"Mrs. Hurley and the snack bar staff, of course." Bernie took the last sip of her orange crush, then lifted the glass high to catch the ice. "We haven't got much time, so we'll have to work fast."

"Time? Time for what?" Shelley was exasperated. "If you three don't tell me what scheme you've cooked up, I'm never talking to any of you ever again as long as I live!"

"Don't you see?" asked Julie, laughing as if it were obvious. "You don't have to get a job. Not when you can start your own catering business."

"Sure," chimed in Bernie. "Once the snack bar starts serving your gourmet treats, they'll have more customers than they know how to handle!"

Shelley began to understand. "You mean sell my desserts?"

"Every week," Nichole told her. "You should make plenty of money, enough to help out your dad."

"And keep your job at Mercy," Julie announced proudly. "You'll be happy. Your dad will be happy." She glanced at the crumbly pie in the center of the table. "And so will everyone at this snack bar!"

Shelley shook her head, smiling gratefully at her friends. "It just might work," she said slowly.

"Might?" Nichole exclaimed. "This plan is *guaranteed*." Then she frowned, remembering the fire Shelley had started in Home Ec. "Unless, of course, you decide to serve your corn soufflé!"

Shelley had caught her friends' excitement. "Don't worry," she assured Nichole, "I'm going to make the richest, most delicious desserts in the world." She stood up, eager to get started. "In fact, I'm going to go home right now and start choosing my recipes!" She grinned, full of her old spunk and fun. "Thanks to you three," she said, "Clarisse may finally shed some of that unsightly fat!"

"It smells scrumptious!" The next day after school, Bernie, carrying a file card covered with greasy thumb prints and Mrs. O'Connor's brownie recipe, walked into the Jansen dining room. She stood there, enjoying the wonderful smells coming from the kitchen. When she looked around her, she hardly recognized the little room where she and Shelley had often done homework on the sturdy oak table.

Julie, whose mother had driven over from East Wood, had brought a white lace tablecloth with her. It made the familiar table look exotic. Laying out matching napkins, Julie stood back to survey her work. "Shelley's invited Mrs. Hurley for dessert and coffee tonight," she told Bernie.

"Tonight?" Bernie asked. "Are you sure that's not too soon?"

Nichole, fussing with flowers and ribbon, was creating a centerpiece for the table. "Don't worry," she told

Bernie airily. "Between this gorgeous table and that heavenly smell, Mrs. Hurley won't be able to resist!"

"I hope not," said Shelley, emerging from the kitchen with a broad smile on her face and a huge tray of pastries in her hands. "Clarisse has already given this evening's menu her seal of approval. Right, Clarisse?"

At the sound of her name, the ancient gray tabby curled on the window seat opened one eye, then closed it again. She was the roundest, most contented cat any of the girls had ever seen.

"I'm serving glazed strawberry tarts, Shelley told them, ticking each delicacy off on her fingers, "almond baskets with chocolate filling, lemon eclairs, marble up-side-down cake . . ."

"Stop!" begged Julie. "I think I'm drooling!"

". . . applesauce muffins," continued Shelley, "iced pecan bars, and Clarisse's personal favorite, charlotte russe."

"What's charlotte russe?" asked Bernie, hungry and curious.

"It's a cream filling inside a shell of ladyfingers," Shelley told her. "I think I'll try a raspberry filling for Mrs. Hurley."

"I'm dying!" groaned Nichole. "I just gained five pounds listening to you!"

"Do you think she'll like it?" asked Shelley.

"Like it!" Bernie carried the recipe card into the kitchen, following the delicious smells to the stove. "She'll love it. And if she doesn't, call me right away so I can devour the leftovers!"

"Me, too," agreed Julie, slipping into her coat. "I promised I'd meet my mom in town, so I'd better get

101

started." She gave Shelley a big hug, then waved to the others. "Good luck tonight!"

"Thanks for coming, Julie," Shelley said. "Thanks for everything."

"She's terrific," Shelley said, watching Julie head off down the street. "You meet the nicest people being a J.V. That's one reason I hope I don't have to give it up."

"Don't worry," Nichole told her. "You'll be back on duty with us this weekend."

"I sure hope so," Shelley said, sounding just a little less confident than she had. "I told Mrs. Hurley I wanted to discuss a business proposal. But now I'm worried about how to present our idea."

"That's no problem," Bernie told her, sneaking a taste of icing off the side of a cake. "Your cooking will say it all! Now, come on. We've got work to do."

Together, the three girls got out the silverware, coffee cups, and glasses, then stacked a pile of china dessert dishes on one end of the table. Nichole made flowered napkin rings and Bernie sat down with a fountain pen and a sheet of paper. Neatly, she wrote down the names of all Shelley's desserts, just like a real restaurant menu, then in pretty scrolled letters at the top she wrote, *Shelley's Catering—At Your Service*. She held the page up to her friends. "What do you think?" she asked.

Shelley studied the elegant menu, then looked at the beautifully set table. She imagined it filled with the rest of the desserts she'd made. She imagined Mrs. Hurley taking her first bite of charlotte russe. "It's perfect," she told Bernie. "It's just too perfect for words!"

When Shelley called Bernie after dinner that night, her voice was so happy that even Mr. O'Connor noticed.

"It's Shelley," he told Bernie as he handed her the phone. "And she sounds like she's swallowed about three canaries!"

"I'll take it upstairs, Dad," Bernie said, then raced to the second floor, stretching the cord from the hall phone into her room and closing the door. "Well?" she asked, breathless, when her father had hung up.

"Well, it worked," Shelley bubbled. "Mrs. Hurley said she'd never tasted better desserts in her whole life." She sighed happily. "In her *whole life*, Bernie!"

"That's great," Bernie said, thrilled. "What about Mercy?"

"That's the best part. Mrs. Hurley is sure the snack bar will want to be a regular customer of Shelley's Catering!" Shelley paused for a second, then rushed on, breathless. "And guess what? She's giving a birthday party for her son next week, and she wants *me* to make the cake!"

"Another customer already! Oh, Shell!" Bernie felt warm and happy and relieved all at once.

"Dad says with the money I'll earn, we can manage without my taking another job." Bernie collapsed contentedly on her bed. She loved stories with happy endings! "He says he's glad I have the chance to do what I love. Isn't it too wonderful, Bern?"

"It sure is," agreed Bernie, staring up at her ceiling stars. They were gleaming faintly in the twilight. "Now if we could just get Roger to feel the same way about Mercy, things would be perfect."

"He's still not speaking to you?" asked Shelley. "I hope I didn't make things worse by telling him off the other day."

"How could you make things worse?" asked Bernie.

103

"They were already as bad as they could be." She remembered the way Roger had snubbed her, walking by without a word every day this week. Things had worked out so well for Nichole and Shelley. Why couldn't she have a happy ending, too?

"Maybe if Roger has a good game tomorrow, he'll stop being mad at the world," Shelley suggested. "You are going to the game, aren't you?"

"Sure," Bernie told her. "In fact, we've got two games to go to. Don't forget, Blake is playing against our varsity."

"Great!" Shelley sounded happy enough for both of them. "I can't wait to see him again. In fact, I can't wait for Sunday when we'll all be on duty together!"

Bernie remembered Roger's angry remark about her "date" with Blake. "I invited Roger to meet Blake tomorrow," she told Shelley, "but he didn't want to. In fact," she confessed, "he practically hung up on me."

"So that's it!" Shelley exclaimed. "He's jealous, Bernie, that's all. If he's any kind of a friend, he'll wake up and realize what a jerk he's being. Just give it time."

"You sound like my mother," Bernie laughed.

"You wait and see," Shelley promised confidently. "Everything will be fine. See you tomorrow!"

"Okay, Shell," Bernie said sitting, gathering up the phone. "Sleep tight."

"Sure. And, Bern?"

"Yes?"

"There weren't any leftovers, but I'm giving a charlotte russe party for my fellow volunteers next week!"

"Gee, that sounds great. Reserve my seat, will you?"

"You bet. And, Bern?"

104

"Yes?"

"Thanks."

The next day was chilly and bright, a perfect day for a football game. But the Ridge Dale bleachers weren't even half full when Bernie met her friends for the JV match. "It's a good thing we're here early," Shelley said, making room for Bernie in between herself and Nichole. "These stands will be overflowing for the varsity game!"

"I see why Roger keeps asking us to come to his games," Bernie had to admit. "It can't be much fun to play without fans."

"Or without decent cheerleading," Nichole added, her eyes fastened on the figure of a blond girl in the middle of the JV cheering squad. "I swear," she said, "that Sheila Forest is positively the most uncoordinated cheerleader on the face of the earth!"

Bernie and Shelley were used to hearing Nichole make fun of Sheila. "You'd think she'd at least take the time to learn the cheers before she got on the field," Nichole continued. "Why, that overweight phoney doesn't even know her left foot from her right!"

Bernie laughed, admiring the way all the girls on the squad performed. They put their arms around each other's waists, kicking high and coming down all together. "Give me an R!" the cheerleading captain yelled into a megaphone. Bernie dug her mittenless hands deep in her pockets and yelled with the rest of the small crowd, her breath making white clouds in the sharp air. "R!" they screamed across the field.

"Give me an I!" the captain yelled again, and Bernie watched the cheerleaders turn cartwheels. She forgot

105

how cold she was, leaping to her feet with the others. "I!" the crowd roared. She heard the band practicing for the varsity game on the field behind them, she smelled hot dogs cooking in the food stand outside the Student Union. It felt good to be out, to be cheering for her team, for her friend!

As the cheer ended, she saw both JV football squads run onto the field. "Give me an E!" the cheerleaders yelled all together, cupping their hands. "E!" the crowd roared back.

"What have you got?" asked the cheerleaders, leaning forward, urging on the crowd. "Ridge Dale!" screamed Bernie and Shelley and Nichole, clapping hard as the referee blew his whistle and a tall, familiar figure fell back from the Ridge Dale front line, the ball raised above his head.

Roger hurled the ball downfield, sending it in a looping arc towards a Ridge Dale player headed for the Hayward goal. The Ridge Dale fans got to their feet, cheering lustily until the ball carrier was brought down by a Hayward tackle. "Wow!" said Shelley, "that was some pass Roger threw!"

"It sure was!" Bernie agreed. "We're in really great position now." She turned happily to her friend. "Maybe you were right, Shell. Maybe everything will work out."

"Just as long as we don't have to sit through another cheer by Sheila the Klutz," added Nichole. "Oh, no," she groaned, pointing to the ref. "Hayward's called a time out. Here they come again!"

It was true. The eight girls on the JV cheering squad filed back onto the field and spread out along the sidelines, ready to do another cheer. "Look at those legs, will you?'' whispered Nichole. ''Someone should do her a favor, and tell her blue is definitely not her color!''

But Bernie wasn't looking at the cheerleaders anymore. Instead, her eyes met those of the JV quarterback just as he walked back behind the bench to get a drink of water. Roger looked up to the stands where Bernie and her friends were sitting. When he saw them, his face broke out in a smile and he waved! He looked happy and proud.

Bernie waved back, hoping he'd meant his smile for her. Hoping that everything was forgiven. ''Did you see that, Shelley?'' she asked. ''Or did I make it up?''

''No, you didn't,'' Shelley said beside her. ''It looks like Roger wants to be friends again, huh?''

''It sure does,'' Bernie said happily, watching Roger head back to the coach and his team. She saw him turn once more and wave toward the stands again. Then she saw him, still looking up at the stands, trip on a first aid box by the sidelines and fall with a sickening thud against the bench! ''No!'' Bernie screamed as if she could stop Roger's body from toppling toward the ground. ''No!''

Suddenly, the field emptied and players from both teams were standing over Roger, who lay on the ground. Bernie held her breath. ''What's wrong?'' she heard people around her in the stands asking. ''What's happened?''

''The quarterback's down,'' a man behind them said. ''Tripped over his own feet.''

Bernie felt angry. She wheeled around to look at the man, but Shelley and Nichole put their arms around her. ''Just relax,'' Shelley told her. ''It's going to be okay.''

107

"Look!" Nichole said now, pointing to the field. "He's moving!"

Sure enough. The three of them could see Roger's hand raised now, the coach and a doctor bending down to him. Suddenly, over the noise and confusion around them, Bernie heard the scream of an ambulance. Then, as Roger was lifted onto a stretcher and carried off the field, Shelley pointed to the sleek white truck that pulled up behind the stands. On the door in red letters were the words, MERCY HOSPITAL—EMERGENCY.

The girls looked on in shock as the stretcher was lifted onto the ambulance, the doors slammed shut, and the siren started up again. The three of them sat numbly in the stands as the ref blew his whistle and the game resumed.

"How can they go on playing, as if nothing's happened?" asked Shelley in disbelief.

"If only he hadn't waved at us!" Bernie shook her head, hot tears starting up in her eyes. "If only we hadn't come to the game!"

Nichole stared into the distance behind them, as the ambulance made its way toward Mercy. She wished she could comfort Bernie, but she didn't know how. She put a timid hand on her shoulder. "At least he's in good hands," she said quietly.

10

The New Volunteer

Bernie and her friends didn't stay to watch Blake Willard and the Hayward varsity defeat Ridge Dale 23-18. Instead, they rushed back to Bernie's house to call Roger's parents. In the O'Connors' roomy kitchen, Bernie's mother was helping Mathew iron fall leaves between sheets of waxed paper. She was used to Bernie bringing visitors home, but not to watching them pass by the kitchen without taking sodas out of the refrigerator or raiding the cupboard for snacks. "What's the hurry?" she asked, as the three girls raced past on their way upstairs.

Bernie walked back and looked in the kitchen door. When Mrs. O'Connor saw her daughter's face, she put the iron down and sent Mathew outside for more leaves. "What's wrong?" she asked, as Bernie's little brother squeezed by them and scooted out the front door.

"It's Roger," Bernie told her mother. "He was hurt at the game."

Mrs. O'Connor looked alarmed. "That's awful," she said. "Is it serious?"

"We don't know. We're going to call his house." Bernie remembered the confusion on the field. "Mom," she said, "they took him away in an ambulance!"

"Quarterback's a rough position," Mrs. O'Connor said as Mathew came back with a fistful of bright yellow and red leaves. "I hope he's all right."

"He wasn't hurt playing football," Bernie admitted. "You know Roger. He was just waving to us, that's all." She looked stricken, recalling how Roger's change of mood had brightened her day. "He wasn't watching where he was going." She bit her lip, trying not to cry.

Mrs. O'Connor opened her arms and Bernie stepped into them, the way she had ever since she was a little girl. But there were some problems her mother's hugs couldn't make better. "I have to go call," she said, brushing the tears from her eyes. "I'll let you know as soon as I hear anything."

Upstairs in her room, with Nichole and Shelley beside her, Bernie dialed Roger's number. Over and over. "There's no answer," she told her friends at last. "I guess everyone's still at the hospital."

As the three wondered what to do next, the phone in Bernie's lap rang loudly. Nervously, she picked it up, smiling with relief at the familiar voice on the other end. "Julie!" she said. "Where on earth are you?"

"I just got off duty," Julie told her. "Cliff and I work at Mercy on Saturdays. And they brought in one of your JV players as we were signing out at one o'clock."

"That's Roger!" Bernie told her. "He's our friend, Roger Thornton. How is he, Julie?"

"Probably pretty groggy," Julie reported. "Mrs. Hurley said they gave him a shot to set his arm."

"Set his arm?" Bernie repeated, while Nichole and Shelley leaned closer, trying to hear.

"Yep. He broke it when he fell. They're keeping him overnight for observation, but it sounds like he'll be fine."

"Thanks, Julie. Thanks a lot. See you next week."

Bernie hung up the phone and collapsed on her bed. Her two friends were dying to hear the news, so she filled them in as best she could. "I guess it'll be okay," she decided. "But Roger's going to be pretty miserable. Football means everything to him."

"Not everything," Nichole teased. "I bet his eyes will light up when he sees a certain J.V. tomorrow."

"That's right!" remembered Shelley. "We're all on duty tomorrow. But if only one of us can work on Ortho, we'll tell Mrs. Hurley it should be you, Bernie." Her own eyes lit up. "After all, I've got a boyfriend of my own waiting for me in Peeds!"

Bernie smiled, remembering the way Jason, the little tonsilectomy patient, had promised to wait for Shelley. "I guess it doesn't really matter who works on Ortho," she said. "Just as long as we can visit Roger. I have a feeling our ex-jock is going to need a lot of cheering up!"

Bernie was relieved to see Blake's friendly smile when all four volunteers signed in at Mercy's Volunteer Office the next morning. "You missed a great game," he told the girls. "Well, maybe not for Ridge Dale," he added, apologetically. "Still, I was really hoping I'd see you afterwards."

All three girls hurried to explain. "Gee, Blake," said Nichole, "we wanted to watch you."

"Yes," added Shelley, "it's just that one of our friends was hurt in the JV game."

"He's right here at Mercy," Bernie told him. "In fact, if you're assigned to Ortho, we'd really like you to say hi to him for us."

"I think you can say hi yourself, Bernie," Mrs. Hurley said, walking up beside them. She checked two names off on her clipboard, then turned to the J.V.'s. She smiled at Shelley and Nichole. "Pediatrics has put in a special request for Shelley, and we've got a backlog of arrangements waiting for our floral specialist in the Flower Room.

"It seems Ortho is still short-handed, so I'm going to send two of my most responsible volunteers up there. Okay, Blake? Bernie?"

"You bet, Mrs. Hurley," Blake told her.

But Bernie wasn't so sure. Of course, she had hoped she'd be assigned to Ortho—but she hadn't counted on working there with Blake.

"Bernie?" Mrs. Hurley was waiting.

How would Roger react to Bernie and Blake walking in together? She glanced at her new friend, tall and handsome in his maroon blazer. Would their visit hurt more than it would help? She looked at Mrs. Hurley. "Sure," she said, smiling uncertainly. "We're on our way."

When the elevator let them out at the Ortho unit, Blake and Bernie reported to the floor nurse. She was a small, wiry woman, full of nervous energy. "Thank goodness you're here," she told them. "We're way behind on lunch menus, and I need a million things from Supplies." She handed Blake a list, then before they could ask her for Roger's room number, she was on her way down the hall. "Oh," she added, turning back after a few steps, "see if you can do anything with Mr. Grump in 210. He thinks he's the only patient in the place!"

Blake and Bernie looked at each other, then laughed. "I guess Roger will have to wait," Bernie said. "I'll help you with Supplies if you give me a hand with Mr. Grump."

"Deal," Blake agreed as they hurried to room 210. Just as they reached the door, a flustered nurse walked out. "Honestly!" she said, brushing past them. "I only have two hands!"

"Well, you're lucky," an irritable voice from inside the room called after her. "I only have one."

"This could be a real challenge," Blake whispered to his friend as they walked briskly into the dark room. "Excuse me," he said, standing beside the curtain which was drawn around the window bed. "We're junior volunteers here. The nurses are shorthanded today. Is there anything we can do to help?"

"There sure is," replied the patient from behind the curtain. "Get some light in here. It feels like I'm in the twilight zone."

Blake laughed, but Bernie shook her head. "Wait a minute," she said as Blake opened the window blinds, filling the room with morning sun. "That grumpy voice sounds awfully familiar." She pulled the privacy curtain aside to reveal Roger, his arm in a plaster cast, lying on his side in the bed.

113

"Bernie?" Roger's face lit up as he stared in disbelief at the pretty redhead in the striped uniform. "Is it really you?"

"Gosh, I'm glad you're all right!" Bernie couldn't hide her delight. "I was so worried when I saw the ambulance take you away."

"To tell you the truth," Roger admitted, "so was I." He turned over, then tried to lift himself up on one arm to greet his visitors. "But I guess everything's going to be okay."

"Here," offered Blake, stepping forward and operating the controls on the bed, "let's get you up where you can see." Slowly, the back of the bed adjusted until Roger was sitting comfortably upright.

"Thanks," said Roger. "It sure is hard without a right hand." He lowered his gaze, studying the long white cast that kept his lower arm and hand pinned straight against his side. "It really makes you mad when you can't do anything for yourself, when you have to ring for someone to help you every two seconds." He looked at the call button on a console by his bed. "Ever since my family left last night, I can't even get a glass of water. I've been pushing that button all morning, but no one seems to care."

"They're really shorthanded in Ortho today," Bernie explained. "The floor nurse told us they've got three new patients on the floor, all in guarded condition."

"That means they need constant attention," Blake added, striding over to the nightstand, pouring a glass of fresh water and setting it on Roger's bed tray. "Their condition could be life-threatening."

"And that's why we're here," Bernie explained, leaning over to straighten Roger's blanket, clearing away

114

the pile of sports magazines and candy wrappers that had accumulated at the bottom of his bed. "We can make sure you're comfortable, while the nurses take care of patients who really need them."

Roger looked at the two volunteers sheepishly. "Guess I've been a pest around here, huh?"

"The nurses nicknamed you Mr. Grump," Bernie told him, laughing. "Does that give you a clue?"

"Hey, it isn't easy being in a cast," sympathized Blake. "I shattered my wrist wrestling once."

Roger brightened. "You're a wrestler?" he asked Blake.

Bernie took a deep breath. It's now or never, she thought. "He sure is," she told Roger. "And a football player, too." She smiled and brought Blake around to the side of the bed. "Roger, this is Blake Willard, Hayward's varsity captain and one of Mercy's best J.V.'s."

Roger's mouth dropped open as he studied Blake's smiling face and broad, rugged shoulders. Finally, to Bernie's surprise, he tried to shake Blake's hand with his own right hand. Then, frowning at the cast he'd forgotten already, he reached over with his left hand. "Hi," he grinned. "You really creamed us yesterday. My dad left me a tape of the game. You lead one mean defense, Blake."

"At least until next year," Blake told him. "Looks like you have some real talent coming up from the JV." He smiled at Roger. "I hear that was some pass you threw in the first quarter. Too bad we got rough on the next play."

"You didn't," Roger told him. "I wasn't hurt in the game." He looked at Bernie and winked. "I just tripped over my own feet."

115

"Roger's too quick and too good to get hurt on the field," Bernie announced, smiling proudly.

"Yeah," Roger added, "I save all my dumb plays for the sidelines. And lately," he added, "I've been making a lot of them." His gray eyes stared at his pretty friend, full of apology. "I hope I can set things straight, Bernie." Then he added hopefully, "It's not too late for apologies, is it?"

Bernie felt a flood of relief. It was good to have one of her very best friends back. And good to know that Roger and Blake actually liked each other! "Of course not," she told him warmly.

"Since this patient seems to have what he needs to cheer him up," Blake said, taking the floor nurse's list and turning toward the door, "I better get to Supplies. Can you start handing out the menus, Bernie?"

"Sure," Bernie said as her fellow J.V. headed down the hall. "And I'll hand my first one out right here." She put a pink menu slip into Roger's left hand. "What's for lunch, Mr. Grump?"

"Funny," said Roger, smiling up at her. "I don't feel grumpy, anymore. I feel hungry!"

"That's a good sign," Bernie told him. She put a pencil on his bed tray. "While you're making your selections, I'll hand out the rest of these menus and be right back."

But she wasn't right back. After she distributed the other menus, Bernie had to help transport a patient to the Operating Room. Next, Blake collected the lunch orders while she set to work making up a whole floor of beds. One job led to another, and by the time she finally poked her head in Roger's door again, it was lunch time and her tour of duty was nearly over.

"You're just in time to join me for lunch," Roger invited. He leaned over the meal Blake had left on his bed tray. "Hmmmm!" he said, looking at the mashed potatoes, peas, and meat loaf he'd ordered. "Never mind all those jokes about hospital food. This smells terrific!"

He picked up his fork with his left hand and tried to scoop up some peas. All but two peas fell off the fork, and when he tried to lift the fork to his mouth, he hit his cheek instead. He looked up to find Bernie stifling a laugh, her hand tight over her mouth. "This isn't as easy as it looks!" he admitted, grinning foolishly. "I guess I could use some help here."

The red-haired volunteer nodded and took the spoon from Roger's tray. She stood close beside him and deftly slipped a spoonful of peas into his mouth. "How's that?" she asked.

Roger smiled up into her green eyes. "Great," he said. "In fact, I could get used to eating like this all the time."

Bernie laughed, feeding him a spoonful of mashed potatoes and gravy. "Oh, no you don't" she warned. "Once you're well and back in school, you're on your own. I'm not going to do this in the cafeteria!"

"Okay, but it might take me a long time to recover," Roger teased, then opened wide for meat loaf.

"Hey, wait!" a friendly voice called from the door. "Let me help, I'm an expert at feeding left-handers."

Bernie and Roger looked up to see Shelley, with Nichole and Blake, standing outside the room. All three J.V.'s wore broad grins and Nichole carried an armload of bright flowers. "These are for our injured football star," she announced, walking in and setting the bouquet on Roger's dresser.

117

"And I've got dessert," Shelley added, following behind her, placing a snack bar sundae on the bed tray. "It's not Charlotte russe," she told Roger, "but we just got off duty, so I didn't have time for anything fancy."

"Looks great to me," Roger said happily, as Shelley scooped the cherry off the top of the sundae and popped it in his mouth. "A very special patient of mine just checked out and left this behind," she added, winking at Bernie.

"Jason!" exclaimed Bernie. "How is he?"

"His parents are back, and they picked him up just a few minutes ago," Shelley reported. "I wheeled him down to discharge, and I got a great big kiss goodbye."

"And *I* delivered flowers to two whole units," said Nichole, collapsing into a chair. "My aching feet tell me it's quitting time."

"And time for a visit," Blake smiled. "We're not allowed to make personal visits on duty, but I'd really love to see that game tape now that we're off—if it's okay with you, Roger."

"Okay?" asked Roger. "It's more than okay. In fact," he said, smiling gratefully at his four visitors, "you're all more than okay. You're great." Embarrassed, he studied his sheets, unable to meet their eyes. "I've been a real jerk."

"You sure have," agreed Nichole. "But we forgive you." She stretched her tired toes, leaning back in the chair. "In fact, we'll even let you back in our lunch club."

"Thanks." Roger beamed. "I don't know why I acted so crazy. It just seemed like your being volunteers was breaking up our group." He looked at the friendly

118

faces around him. "I didn't realize how important what you do is," he told them. "But I sure found out—the hard way."

"Boy," said Shelley, "I wish Teddy were here to film this happy ending."

"Why not film it for him?" Roger tried to sit up, then pointed to the dresser. "My dad left the video camera in that top drawer."

"Great," offered Blake. "I'll shoot you guys signing Roger's cast." He handed around pens, then took the camera out of the drawer and aimed it at Roger and the three girls.

As his friends giggled and gathered around him, scrawling their names on the slippery cast, Roger shook his head. "Wow! I still can't believe how stupid I was," he told Bernie. "What if you'd let me change your mind? What if you'd decided not to become a J.V.?"

Bernie grinned at him with affection. "Not a chance!" she said, signing her name with a little heart over the *i* in Bernie, then making a goofy face into the camera. "Hi, Teddy!" she called, waving to their absent friend.

"Seriously, Bernie," said Roger. "I'm really sorry. I only wish there were some way I could make it up to you all."

"There is!" Bernie told him, winking at the others. "On behalf of J.V.'s everywhere," she told Roger, picturing how cute her friend would look in one of Mercy's maroon blazers, "there's always room for one more!"